The Return of the O'Connells
Paperback Copyright © 2022 Lorhainne Ekelund
Editor: Talia Leduc

ISBN-13: 978-1998775187

Give feedback on the book at:
lorhainneeckhart@hotmail.com

Twitter: @LEckhart
Facebook: AuthorLorhainneEckhart

Printed in the U.S.A

The Return of the O'Connells

THE O'CONNELLS
BOOK ELEVEN

LORHAINNE ECKHART

About the O'Connells

The O'Connells of Livingston, Montana, are not your typical family. Follow them on their journey to the dark and dangerous side of love in a series of romantic thrillers you won't want to miss. Raised by a single mother after their father's mysterious disappearance eighteen years ago, the six grown siblings live in a small town with all kinds of hidden secrets, lies, and deception. Much like the contemporary family romance series focusing on the Friessens, this romantic suspense series follows the lives of the O'Connell family as each of the siblings searches for love.

The O'Connells

The Neighbor
The Third Call
The Secret Husband
The Quiet Day
The Commitment, An O'Connell Novella
The Missing Father
The Hometown Hero
Justice
The Family Secret
The Fallen O'Connell
The Return of the O'Connells
And The She Was Gone
The Stalker
The O'Connell Family Christmas
The Girl Next Door
Broken Promises
The Gatekeeper
The Hunted

This time, it could come from within, as a shadowy new enemy has found its way into the close-knit family and could ultimately destroy the bond the siblings share, forcing them to finally cut their losses and walk away from one another.

CHAPTER

One

There was something about secrets: They had a way of making themselves felt long before anyone even learned of them. The O'Connells kept secrets, and they were good at that. It seemed they always had—from others, from each other. But secrets had a way of slipping out explosively, scandalously, and never without repercussions. That left the kinds of battle scars the average person couldn't see.

The O'Connells had two kinds of secrets. There was the kind they wanted to keep, but there was also the kind they wouldn't dare tell a soul, the kind that had to stay secret forever.

Now Karen had another secret of her own as she sat quietly in the passenger side of Jack's Mercedes, anything but the dutiful and obedient wife.

"You've said not two words since we left the office," Jack said. There was something about the way he spoke to her, the edge, like an alpha. The way he watched her at times, she knew he wondered what she was keeping from him.

She took in the barren trees of another season settling upon them, the frigid dirty white packed at the sides of the freshly plowed roads, the exhaust from the vehicles ahead of them. She'd seen it all thousands of times before, except now it was as if she were seeing everything for the first time.

What was different?

Everything. The phone call.

She pulled in a breath and glanced over to Jack, reminding herself that she needed to tell him, but again the words wouldn't come. "Have a lot on my mind," she replied.

He only nodded, but she could feel the weight of something being held back. Was it her, or was it him? She forced herself to glance back to Brady, who was staring out the side window. His dark hair needed a cut. He glanced back down to his phone, thumbing over the screen. There was something on his mind, too.

"Brady, you too haven't said much, either," Jack said, lifting his gaze to the rear-view mirror as he pulled up to the lights. "How was school today?"

"School's school," he replied. "What do you want me to say? I was given the option to take some elective courses to finish the school year with the other kids, because the only class I wanted is full, but I said hell no. I'm finishing the required math, and then I have enough credits and I'm out of there." He swiped his hands together. Could she blame him? "Is Luke coming back?"

Right. That was the other call she'd had.

Karen turned back to looking straight ahead, out the windshield, seeing the street she knew like the back of her hand, feeling the comfort of her husband's vehicle despite how different everything seemed. "Yes, he called this morning."

"And what did he say, again? That he's bringing someone?" Jack said.

She needed to pull in another breath, feeling the tightness in her chest and the heaviness that settled inside her again. "He said it was an accidental kiss with consequences, and he wants us to meet her, which is apparently his way of saying he met someone he really likes and is bringing her home with him to meet the family. This should be interesting."

"And he's going to be at Ryan's?" Brady said, a hopeful note in his voice.

She made herself look back at him, seeing something else in his expression. Right, Luke was his buddy, the brother he leaned on to keep his head straight, even though he was the one who was often gone at a moment's notice.

"No, Marcus's," she said, then realized maybe she'd forgotten to relay that text.

Jack shook his head. "You forgot to mention that," he said, the edge in his voice slipping into that pissed-off tone he seemed to have been taking with her more and more as of late.

She made herself drag her gaze over to him, taking in the beard that had been growing in for three days now. He was settling into a look that was more messy bad boy than his usual classy style. She wondered if he had any idea. Likely not.

"Marcus lives just across the street from Ryan, so I'm at a loss to understand how that's a big deal," she said. "Besides, it was just a text. Do I need to report every single thing to you?" Even she didn't miss the sharpness in her voice, and for a moment she was positive Jack gripped the steering wheel that much harder.

"You two aren't going to start fighting again, are you?" Brady jumped in.

She had to remind herself he was the newest member of their family, her brother. Brady was perceptive, quiet, polite, and kept everything to himself, still finding his place among the O'Connells.

"We don't fight, Brady. Do we, Jack?" she said, and she didn't miss the rude sound Jack made in response as he pulled into Marcus's driveway and parked behind Charlotte's Subaru. The sheriff's car was parked out front, so she didn't need to wonder whether Marcus was still at work.

Jack took his time putting the car in park and turning off the engine, then gave everything to her with that one look. His icy blue eyes could hide things from her that she would've had no idea about. "We fight," he said. "You fight. Brady's right."

A smile tugged at Brady's lips as he climbed out of the car without saying a word and closed the back door, and she and Jack followed.

"Brady, it's called having a difference of opinion and standing your ground," she called out to Brady's back, as he was halfway to the house.

He didn't turn around as he kept walking, only lifted his hand and tossed out over his shoulder, "If that's what you want to call it, but I know fighting when I hear it—and I know not to ever take you on."

Then he was up the steps, and she found herself taking in Jack as she walked around the vehicle, pulling at her red coat, feeling the cold on her face, feeling the ice under her impractically high black boots.

"Careful," Jack said. "It seems Marcus needs to clear this snow better."

She didn't look over as she pressed her hand on the

hood of the car, taking careful steps, but Jack walked around and offered his arm. He was almost the perfect gentleman, always there for her, though he never saw her point of view on anything.

"Marcus has a lot on his plate," she said. "And Brady really thinks we're fighting?"

Jack was walking carefully, holding on to her, until they reached the sidewalk, which had been cleared of snow. The cold bit her bare thighs over her impractical knee-high boots, and the early winter wind whipped under her dress.

"We do fight, Karen, or rather, you do."

There it was, her need to set him straight. "Really?" she said. "Because how I see it is that you try to tell me what to do, and you never ask my opinion on anything before deciding, thinking you can just go and do whatever you want, whenever you want. Just know that I will never let you tell me what to do, and I'll never go along with something just because you can't be bothered to ask and check in with me. I honestly believe you expect me to just fall in line with your way of thinking…"

"So you disagree and argue just because, Karen? I often wonder if you'd ever just go along with something because I decided it was best or because you understand that I'm looking out for you. No! You make nothing easy." It came out quite sharply, and she could feel the passion in him.

The way he said it, Karen could feel something more coming. "You mean I don't make it easy for you to steamroll me."

"No, I mean we're married," he said. "You're my wife, Karen, even with everything this family has been through, all the secrets and lies. Maybe I just want a little peace for us, a little of you meeting me halfway, instead of feeling as if everything is a fight." He stopped at the bottom of the steps and faced her, pulling in a breath. When he let it out, she could see his frustration.

The inside door was still open, and they should've headed in, but Jack had something else on his mind. His expression had an edge, a hardness. He was distracted. She wondered what secret he was keeping. As she stared at the man she loved, she wondered whether this discontent would always exist between them.

"You know something, don't you?" she said, hearing the accusation in her voice. "You did something."

"My name's been tossed out to run for governor. I'm on the ticket."

There it was, the surprise she didn't want.

Jack glanced away a second and then back to her. "You knew it was coming, and so did I. I just didn't expect it now."

"That means…"

"I think you know what it means, Karen. We have to leave Livingston, and we'll have to close up shop on the law practice."

She just stared, feeling a heaviness settle right in her stomach, leaving her with that sick feeling that wouldn't go away. "I see," she said, and then she said nothing else, because this was just something she didn't want on her plate right now. She found herself turning to the steps to walk away, but his hand was on her, and he was right in her space, holding her so she couldn't leave.

"Don't do that," he said. "Don't just walk away. You think I don't get that you're pissed off and you don't want this? Neither do I, but you know about the favors I called in to fix things, to clean up after all those damn secrets your family had, to keep Marcus as sheriff and keep the vultures from our door. So is this how you're going to handle it? Because I'm not in the mood for you to dig your heels in and not give an inch."

She shook her head. "You're way off base, Jack. I don't care right now about the governor ticket, and I don't want to think about it or start asking you all the things I'm wondering, like why you couldn't bother telling me until now. Will there always be something that falls into that category where you think you don't need to tell me every-thing? Anyway, no, I'm not there yet, because I have stuff going on, too."

He was confused and unimpressed. "What the hell are you talking about, Karen? What stuff—work or something personal, more secrets, something with your family?"

Oh, great, he was really going down that road again. He stepped back and was no longer touching her, but the early Montana winter cold was starting to sting a bit, and she supposed now was as good a time as any.

"No, no, and no," she said. "The doctor's office called me."

When a smile touched his lips, she forced herself to pull it together and continue.

"Don't get excited. They confirmed I was pregnant, but I lost the baby."

There it was. His expression filled with the same thing she hadn't been able to feel.

"Right," she said, then gestured with her thumb behind her. "I'm going in."

She started up the steps, and when she pulled open the door and glanced back to Jack, who was still standing there, staring out at nothing, she didn't have a clue what the hell he was thinking.

CHAPTER

Two

Charlotte's cheeks had really plumped out. Marcus wasn't sure why he noticed that today, maybe because he could see her discomfort in the way she walked with her hand on her lower back before sliding onto a stool at the island. He heard Alison on the stairs with Eva, evidently going up, and moved around to his wife.

"You okay there, babe?" he said, surveying the jicama and red peppers, her favorites of late, along with sour cream, oranges, and sardines. He picked up the knife and took in the broccoli and cauliflower, as well, knowing she wanted it all chopped.

"Yeah, just cramping, is all, and my feet are aching. Not sure this is much better. I'm tired and just damn uncomfortable. Sorry, don't mean to complain." She made a face, letting out a breath that took some effort. But then, everything had been taking more effort lately: sleeping, getting up, moving, even driving, as she couldn't seem to get close enough to reach the pedals anymore.

"You get to complain," he said. "You know I'd carry

the baby for you, but it's not possible. Just sit there, and I'll finish this. You should really stay home tomorrow. I'll put Colby on the phones and get him to look after things, and I'll have a talk with Alison about her doing more over here for you, helping with Eva, doing the laundry."

Charlotte lifted a brow, and he took her in. She had her hair pulled back and was wearing one of his white and blue T-shirts, considering they had passed the point where she could even button up her deputy shirt. She was moving a lot slower, and he wasn't sure he wanted her in the office at this point.

"When the baby comes, you know you can't get by with just Colby," she said. "I know we haven't talked about this, but we need to discuss bringing someone in temporarily."

The way she said it, he knew she was getting to the heart of the discussion he'd been putting off.

"About that," he said, not missing the way she stiffened, "we haven't really talked about the next step, likely because of everything that's happened with the family. Seems it's been one disaster averted after another. But we need to." He made a point of setting the knife on the wooden cutting board and leaned on the island, hearing a car pull up outside and knowing they'd be invaded by his family any moment.

"Marcus…"

He reached over and touched her arm, then ran his hand up, over her shoulder, and back down before pulling back and picking up the knife again. "No, let me finish. We need to talk about this now because this baby is coming soon, very soon, and you're going to be home here—and maybe that doesn't need to be temporary."

The way she hesitated, he could see she wasn't about to take this well.

"Charlotte, I need you to listen to me, okay? You know

I need to bring someone in now to handle everything you do, and you're right that I've put off talking to you about this because of everything that's been going on, but I can't anymore. I'm the sheriff, and the city council have also put it out there."

He thought back on his discussion with the mayor and council members, who had said with no political correctness whatsoever that it was time to hire a woman to take over for Charlotte, because she was pregnant and would need to stay home. Actually, it had been Jessa, whom Suzanne had once been friends with at school, now married with her own kids, who'd come right out and said Charlotte needed to stay home with her baby so a job could go to someone who needed it. He was still stunned that had slipped past her lips, and two of the men on the council had even flushed red. He'd make sure that part never got back to Charlotte.

"Put what out there, exactly? What are you talking about? I love my job and working…"

"I know, and it's not forever, but you want to be home with the baby after it's born, right?" he said. Why was it that they'd never really taken a moment and talked about this? "And there's Eva, too. With Mom gone and us not knowing when she's coming back…"

"Well, of course I'm not planning on going right back to work, but I never planned on staying home. Eva is in school right now, and Alison can still pick her up like she's been doing. It's not unworkable. You know I love my job and working with you…"

"Yeah, but, Charlotte, with the upcoming election, anything could happen. I could suddenly not be sheriff anymore. It's a possibility, so there's that, too."

That was the other thing they hadn't talked about. He

wondered if it was something she'd been thinking about, by the way she hesitated and let out another breath.

"You're being ridiculous," she said. "You're a shoo-in, and everyone who knows you around here knows you're the best for the job."

All he could do was shake his head. "So much has happened to create doubts in everyone's minds. Come election day, with other names on the ballot, people could be voting for someone else just because that candidate doesn't come with the same baggage. After the scandal, people here are still wondering what the O'Connells are hiding, thinking there has to be something there. I may very well be home with the baby," he teased.

She didn't pull her gaze or smile. "Don't joke about something like that, Marcus. Besides, the election isn't for a while yet, and if anything, this year has been one of a lot of changes and surprises. I shouldn't have to tell you not to jump all the way to the worst-case scenario. Do you want me to stop working and stay home? Is that what you're saying?"

The way she asked, he had to remind himself this was dangerous territory. Just then, he heard the front door and footsteps, and then Brady walked in, went right to the fridge, and opened it and pulled out a beer before twisting off the cap.

"Hold that thought," was all he said to Charlotte as he turned to Brady. "That's as far as that goes, young man." He reached for the beer and took it, seeing something in his younger brother's expression that he recognized all too well.

"I'm eighteen," Brady said. "You know this is ridiculous. Luke lets me have a beer."

From the way Brady said it, with that teenage attitude,

Marcus predicted that he was likely going to point out that he was legally an adult next.

"Really? Now, why don't I believe that?" Marcus said before he lifted the beer, took a swallow, and set it on the counter by the cutting board in front of him. Charlotte was staring long and hard at Brady and then him.

"It's true," Brady said. "Seriously, what's the big deal, anyway?"

What was he supposed to say? When he was Brady's age, he'd been drinking and getting into the kind of trouble he still couldn't believe he'd escaped unscathed. "It is a big deal," Marcus finally said. "So, considering I'm the sheriff and the legal drinking age is twenty-one, try helping yourself to a soda instead. Seriously, Brady—and what's with the face? Something happen today?"

He heard the door and more footsteps, then a thunk, before he spotted Karen, barefoot in a short-sleeved dress. Jack appeared behind her, and he was sure Suzanne and Harold were there now, too.

"Nothing. It's fine," was all Brady said before walking out of the kitchen without helping himself to a soda.

Jack said something to Charlotte, and Karen was in his fridge, pulling out a bottle of white that he hadn't known was in there.

"Hey there, Marcus, can you open the oven?" Suzanne said as she strolled in behind them, carrying a roasting pan covered with tinfoil. "I'll pop this in to warm again." She still wore her heavy bomber jacket, and her hair was hanging long and loose.

"Sure. What is that?" He opened the oven for his sister, spotting Harold, too. His deputy jutted his chin to him and gestured to the living room, where Brady had gone. Maybe he'd have a word with the kid and figure out what was going on with him.

Karen was pouring a big glass of wine, and Jack was still talking to Charlotte, though without pulling his gaze from his wife. Evidently, there was something amiss between the two of them. It had been a while since his sister had had a drink.

"Made lasagna," Suzanne said. "Well, I decided to be creative and made a vegetarian kind. The noodles are zucchini."

"And no meat?" Marcus said, taking in his sister, who he knew had way too much time on her hands.

She pulled a face, and he could hear more voices from the front door—Owen, Tessa, and Ryan, he thought. Suzanne shrugged out of her coat. "Lasagna doesn't always have to have meat in it, you know. Besides, it will be good. There's lots of mushrooms and cheese. You'll never miss it."

"Miss what?" Owen said, and Marcus wondered what he'd say, considering he was mister barbecue, in charge of that part of dinner, which had to always be meat.

"Suzanne made lasagna for us, vegetarian," Marcus said.

The way Owen dragged his gaze from him to Suzanne was almost comical. "Not funny, Suzanne," was all he said.

She just waved her hand and wandered to the fridge before pulling it open and taking out a beer. "Be adventurous, Owen. We don't always have to eat meat."

Ryan and Jenny came in next, and everyone seemed to linger in the kitchen. When he met Jack's eyes, the other man nodded toward the living room.

"Here, take over," Marcus said, handing the knife to Ryan, who only looked at it for a second before Jenny shook her head and stepped in.

"Ryan's useless," she said. "Here, let me."

Marcus stepped away, around Ryan and Charlotte.

Everyone was talking, though the voices of his family faded as he walked out of the kitchen, following Jack into the living room, where Brady and Harold were sitting across from each other, deep in discussion.

"Everything okay?" Marcus said.

Jack appeared dressed down, and Marcus wondered about the new shaggy look he had going on. What was that about, a big case? He didn't think so. Either way, shaving seemed to have been put on the back burner.

"Look, I wanted to give you a heads-up, is all," Jack said. "I just told Karen that I got a call, and my name's been put out there for governor. I knew it was coming, and soon. So there it is—and there's something else."

He just stared down at Jack, who was a few inches shorter than him, knowing he'd made a deal with the devil, so to speak, to save their asses. "I don't know what to say. I'm sorry, considering we had a serious part in this. So the favors have been called in."

"Knew it would come," Jack replied. "At the same time, Karen just dropped a bombshell on me before we walked in. I need to get her out of here. We have something to deal with. Can you keep Brady for the night?"

He heard the sound of a car but couldn't see who it was, as the inside door was closed. "Yeah, Brady can stay. Should I be worried about something between you and my sister?"

Jack hesitated.

Just then, Marcus's phone started ringing, and he pulled it out, seeing an unknown number.

Jack touched his arm. "Take your call," was all he said, then started back to the kitchen, obviously not wanting to talk.

"Marcus here," he said.

Harold looked over to him expectantly and gave him

everything from where he sat, likely because one of them could need to head out now.

"It's Mom," Marcus finally said, shaking his head at Harold, hearing the voices from the kitchen. He leaned against the stairway railing. "Hey, was thinking about you," he said. "How are you and…?"

There was something strange about knowing his mom was with their dad, but he hadn't shared with anyone how unsettled he was about it.

"And your dad, you mean?" she said. "I'm sorry I haven't called, but I wanted to let you know that we're coming back."

He hadn't expected that. Just then, the front door opened, and there was Luke—with a woman who had brown hair and wore a dark coat. It seemed as if it had been one thing after another as of late. Marcus reached over and punched his brother's shoulder playfully, then gestured to the woman before turning away.

"Like now, you mean?" he said. "Are you sure it's okay?" He took in the dark railing going upstairs, knowing Alison and Eva were up there.

"You know what, Marcus? I miss all of you, and Charlotte's due anytime now. I want to be there. I told your dad I was planning on coming myself, but your dad said he was coming, too. Through it all, he misses all of you, and I know he still wants to make so much right. He said he knows how to be careful, to hide, so what am I to say to that?"

He thought he heard something in the background. "Okay, so when? I'll let everyone know."

"No, don't tell anyone. I want it to be a surprise. Listen, that's your dad calling me. I've got to go. Your dad's just working out logistics now, as he said, but I'm hoping a few days, two at the most. Any problems on his end, and I'll come myself."

It would be great to see his mom, but not telling anyone was something he didn't want to do. This family couldn't handle more secrets.

"A surprise, really?" he said. "Don't you think we've had enough? I have to tell Charlotte, at least…"

His mom sighed. "Okay, fine, just don't make a big deal about it."

"So I can tell everyone?"

"Yes, just not the kids, Brady, Alison, Eva. I want to surprise them, and your dad still has some things to work out with Brady because of how everything went down. He still hasn't talked to him."

Right, and then there was that. "No promises," Marcus said. "Call me when you know."

Then he hung up, and he could hear Luke in the kitchen, introducing whoever the woman was.

He had to think about Karen and Jack and whatever was going on with them, too. Maybe now wasn't the time to tell his siblings that their mom was planning on coming back. Luke had brought someone home, Karen and Jack had a problem, and then there was Brady, who'd likely be staying with him and Charlotte that night.

Right, just another evening with the O'Connells.

When he started back to the kitchen, he heard Charlotte say, "I think my water just broke."

"Sorry about this," Luke said, pulling Rosemary aside, as chaos had ensued.

Marcus was on the phone with Charlotte's doctor, and Jenny and Tessa were in the living room with Charlotte, with Owen and Ryan lingering in the background. Charlotte had changed and appeared far too calm now—in his mind, anyways.

Then there was Karen, who was working on her second glass of wine. Something was definitely off with his sister. Jack said something to her, and he could see the lingering tension between them. Alison, Brady, and Eva wandered into the living room, too, uncertain.

He should talk to Brady.

"Don't apologize," Rosemary said. "This is exciting. Your sister-in-law is having a baby today." She ran her hands over his arms and down, though it wasn't cold in the house. "You know what? Maybe this was fate stepping in. So that's the little girl."

Luke glanced over to see that she was watching Eva, and he knew she was having some trouble with the fact that it had been her brother who pointed a gun at her and terrorized her the way he had. Maybe this had suddenly become too real for her. He knew well the kind of dangerous territory he was wading into, so was that just her way of pointing out to him that maybe this wasn't a good idea, her meeting his family? Would they understand?

"They have no idea who I am, do they?" she said. She'd dressed the part today, casual but put together, with wide-legged slacks and a black long-sleeved knit sweater. Her hair was long and loose, with soft waves he loved running his hands through. He wondered now about the wisdom of what he was doing.

"They know you're someone who means a lot to me," he said. "That's all they need to know."

The hint of a smile touched her lips, and she crossed her arms, the tension lingering. It had taken a lot for him to convince her to come.

"So, you two…" Suzanne said, approaching them. "Rosemary, nice to meet you, even under the circumstances. I didn't get a chance to grill you on my brother and how you know him or how long you've known each other—you know, the usual third degree." She glanced between them teasingly. Harold appeared amused as he approached behind her.

"Don't worry about answering, Rosemary," Harold said. "It seems you'll be able to slide in under the radar without the usual O'Connell grilling about every personal detail, considering Charlotte's now taken center stage."

He could see that Rosemary was at a loss for what to say, and Suzanne didn't appear too inclined to let it drop, as she stared long and hard at Rosemary.

"No, seriously, how did you two meet?" she said. She was doing what he would've expected from Karen, who was still in the kitchen, where Jack had taken her wine from her and set it on the counter.

"We actually met in Geneva," she said, and he looked over to her, wondering why. The truth was something she couldn't share.

"It was a while ago," Luke said, jumping in. "She was a girl in the bar. Couldn't take my eyes off her. The rest is history, so to speak. The end."

She nodded, her arms still crossed, and he worried for a moment about what she might decide to add.

"I didn't bring Rosemary here for the third degree, Suzanne," he continued. "Besides, what's going on with Karen and Jack?"

Suzanne turned and glanced over her shoulder. He wasn't sure, by the expression on Harold's face, whether he might know what was going on.

"I haven't had a chance to pull Karen aside and talk," Suzanne said. "She's been like this since we got here not long ago. Some bad news, is all I can think. I haven't seen her this off in a while. You know she and Jack have been trying for a baby."

He just stared for a second. Rosemary was taking in everyone, glancing over to Karen and her husband. He wondered whether he should step in, knowing how Karen was. She held everything in, kept secrets that no one would ever expect.

"No, I didn't know that," he said. "She's drinking, so apparently something's amiss."

"Yeah…" Suzanne breathed out just as Marcus walked over, pocketing his phone.

"I'm taking Charlotte in to the hospital now," he said. "Her doctor's going to meet us there. Her water broke, but she's not having any contractions yet." He seemed rattled. "Ryan and Jenny are going to take Eva, but can you take

Brady? Jack asked if he could stay the night, because something's going on with Karen. He didn't elaborate, though."

"No worries," Luke said. "I've got Brady. You just take care of your wife and that little baby who's about to make an appearance."

Marcus was already walking away, and now Jack somehow had Karen walking toward them. Charlotte was at the door, and Jenny helped her put her shoes on. Marcus was holding her coat. Everyone was so quiet, focused on her.

"Marcus, the bag I packed is upstairs," she said. "Don't forget it."

"I know where it is," Alison called out.

"Go get it," Marcus said, and she ran up the stairs past them.

"I'm so sorry about this, Rosemary," Charlotte said, still unusually calm. "It's nice to meet you. We'll see you again, won't we?"

Marcus had his hand on her back after shrugging on his own coat, and Alison raced back down the stairs, carrying an overnight bag, which Marcus reached for.

"No, don't apologize," Rosemary said. "This is such a happy time for you. Go, go."

Near them, Jack was quietly helping Karen on with her coat after she'd pulled on her high-heeled boots.

"Just give me a second," Luke muttered, setting a hand on Rosemary's arm. She didn't nod as she glanced up to him, and he saw the awkwardness there. Yeah, he'd get her and Brady out of there...and then what? He'd have to touch base with the kid and figure out a way to keep Rosemary from bolting.

Ryan opened the door from outside and called out, "Warmed the car for you."

Luke had stepped over to Jack and Karen. Jack was

pulling on his own coat, and as Luke approached his sister, he saw something in her expression that she couldn't hide. He glanced only a second at Jack, who seemed on edge, before turning back to her. "Hey, what's going on with you?" he said. "Everything okay?"

Karen pressed a hand to his arm. "So that's the girl, is it, Rosemary?" she said. "You should bring her by tomorrow. We can talk, and it'll give me a chance to find out more about her. You said she's from…?"

He was about to say something, but when he glanced over, Jack shook his head, and Luke realized there was way more going on than he knew. "Indiana," he replied. "There's time. Are you two heading home?"

Karen said nothing before touching his arm again and stepping over to Suzanne and Rosemary.

He gave everything to Jack now. "What's going on? Something's wrong." He gestured with his thumb to his sister.

"Yeah, she just dropped a bombshell on me before we came in. I'm taking her to the hospital. She told me she was pregnant and lost the baby. That was all I knew before we walked in here. Listen, you can take Brady, right, since Marcus has to go?"

Luke just shrugged. "Yeah, of course I can. You go take care of my sister, and let me know if I can do something. And thanks for looking out for Brady, keeping him with you. Anything going on I need to know about?"

Jack was pulling his keys from his pocket. "He's struggling a bit. I know he hasn't talked to Raymond at all. Never asked about him, either. Karen tried to bring him up and have a talk last week, but he was very matter of fact when he shut it down. In school, he's brilliant, and he announced he's likely done with his courses. You might have a better chance of getting in his head and finding out what's what. Oh, and I told Marcus already, but my name has been tossed out for governor. Karen and I will have to close up shop here. She'll likely go kicking and screaming, as it seems all the favors I asked are now being called in. Karen's right, though. We should have you over so everyone can have at Rosemary and grill her and pull out all her secrets. You know how you all are in this family."

He knew Jack was trying to keep things light, but he wondered if his stance would change if he only knew who Rosemary's brothers were.

Then Jack stepped away and somehow maneuvered Karen to the door and out. Suzanne and Harold were back in the kitchen, and he thought Tessa and Jenny were washing up dishes or something, while Owen and Ryan were in the living room. It was just him and Rosemary standing in the open hallway.

"You know, maybe we should take this as our cue to go…" Rosemary said.

"Hey, you two, come in here," Owen called out.

Rosemary stiffened, but he reached for her hand and strode with her into the living room.

"So is everyone staying?" he said. He could see headlights outside the window as Marcus and Charlotte pulled away, followed by Jack and Karen. He realized Brady was sitting in a chair in the corner, staring at his phone and thumbing over it as if it held all the answers.

"There is dinner in the oven," Ryan said.

"That's not dinner," Owen cut in. "Suzanne is apparently on a vegetarian kick and made a meat-free lasagna out of zucchini. I think you should order pizza." He turned to take in Rosemary, who was still standing beside Luke, before dragging his gaze back to him. "With all the excitement, Karen and Suzanne didn't get a chance to grill you on details. At least now we can all sit back and listen. So, Rosemary, how did you and Luke meet, how long have you known each other, and where do you live?"

He was surprised Owen had asked, considering he had never been a chatty guy. But then, Luke had never brought a woman home before, either.

Rosemary pulled in a breath, and he could feel her unease, so he cut in and said, "Does it matter? We're just…"

"Actually, I think your family needs to know," Rosemary said. "Just tell them the truth, everything, because it will come out eventually."

He didn't have to look over to his brothers to know they were intrigued, curious, and Rosemary now had all their attention. Even Brady had put down his phone and lifted his gaze, listening to everything.

"What truth?" Ryan said. "What are you talking about?"

"Rosemary, no," Luke said. "This isn't how to handle this, and it's completely irrelevant. They don't need to know."

There was something about Rosemary that he knew well, though: She took a lot of convincing. He could see how bothered she was and how seeing Eva had hit too close to home for her.

"I disagree, Luke," she said. "If it were irrelevant, you and I wouldn't be standing here, debating this, and I wouldn't feel absolutely shitty about being here." She looked right at Owen then, even as Luke went to reach for her arm. "What Luke didn't tell you is that my brother was the one who broke into Marcus's house and held a gun to your mother and that little girl over there. Yes, he's dead, but I feel responsible, even though Luke reminded me I wasn't the one who held the gun. But there it is. Ben

Schwartz was my brother. I live in Indiana. We met in a bar."

All Luke could do now was take in what he could only figure was shock. Owen had a sort of ominous expression he'd never seen before as he slowly slid forward and then stood up. Ryan followed, and for a minute, he feared the worst.

"Well, I guess you're right about one thing, Rosemary: You shouldn't be here," Owen stated so matter of factly, leaning in with passion and anger. He narrowed his gaze at Luke. "You surprise me more than anyone, bringing the enemy here. I'm just glad Marcus and Charlotte left. Seriously, Luke, for you, this is hitting below the belt. I'd never expect this from you."

Rosemary didn't reach for him but stood stoically, taking it as if this was her lot.

"You're out of line," Luke said. "It's not her fault. You can't blame her or hold her responsible for something she didn't do."

Ryan stepped closer just as Eva came running in, and he reached for her and lifted her. "You should take your lady and go," he said, then turned and took Eva out of the living room.

Luke realized maybe he'd been wrong about his family. He merely nodded and glanced down to a shaken Rosemary. "Let's go," he said.

Brady was standing there, evidently unsure of what to say or do.

"You too, there, young man," he said. "You're with us. Grab your things."

He waited only a second as Rosemary and Brady went to the door to put on their shoes and coats, the silence thick and uncomfortable. He turned back to Owen, feeling the kind of distance he'd never experienced before. "You know what, big brother? Just remember what it felt like when everyone in town turned against Mom, against Marcus, again all of us, convicting us of something we hadn't done. Be mindful you don't join a witch hunt against Rosemary. She didn't do anything. She's not responsible for what Ben did."

"What are you doing, Luke?" Owen said. "I hear you that she didn't do it, and I get it, but still. It was her brother, her family. You really surprise me. That was our mom and little Eva. He would have killed them. You can't be involved with her."

"Or what, Owen? Come on. Say it."

Owen seemed to consider something as he glanced away, then shook his head as if working out a kink. "No, Luke, I've said enough, more than I should've had to. What the hell are you thinking? I'm going to say this for everyone in this family: You need to go now, and don't bring her back."

CHAPTER

Four

Raymond had never been one for ballcaps, yet there he was, wearing one, along with rimless glasses that looked real. The beard he'd started to grow was a mix of white and dark, and the name on his passport was Jake Peters.

What surprised Iris more than anything was how easy it had been for him to make a call to get what he needed, step into a new identity, and become someone else. Should she ask for more details about how he had access to the money he did? His only response had been that it was his emergency retirement stash. What that meant, exactly, she had no idea.

"They answer you yet?" he asked.

She didn't know he'd been watching her from where they stood at the airport, waiting for their luggage to slide down the carousel. He had taken up a spot against the back wall and seemed to blend right in.

"I called Marcus and left a message to let him know we were on our way," she said. "Then I called Karen, but she didn't answer, and I didn't leave a message. Owen picked up, and he hadn't heard anything from Marcus, so I have no idea where things are with Charlotte and the baby. She could've had the baby by now, for all I know." She breathed out the last part, keeping her voice low, knowing Raymond was watching everything and everyone, even though it appeared he wasn't.

She took in the man she'd married, the father of her children, and she wondered, if he walked out of her life now, would she be okay this time? As soon as Marcus had texted that Charlotte's water broke and they were on their way to the hospital, Raymond had packed everything and gotten them on the first flight back home, a red-eye, which was likely why she felt miserable now. Who in their right mind would pick a late-night flight anywhere? The only sleep she'd had, sitting upright, had been a few hours leaning against Raymond's shoulder.

Sometimes it felt like she was talking to herself when he didn't answer, as he was doing now. She heard the whir and clunk as their luggage appeared and slid down the conveyor, and he walked over with the luggage cart, reached for her two large suitcases, and tossed them onto the cart as if they weighed nothing. Then he reached for his smaller brown canvas bag and nodded toward her, already walking.

"You tell Owen we're back?" he said, his voice low.

She walked with him, keeping up with his pace, which was fast and cautious as they strode to the rental car carousel. "No, I didn't say anything, just asked about Charlotte. Marcus is the only one I told, but I didn't tell him when, just like you asked, even though I don't understand the need for secrecy with the kids."

He said nothing else as they stopped at the counter and filled out paperwork. She took in his California driver's license, also in the name of Jake Peters, as well as his credit card. She should ask him how, but there were things about all of this that she really didn't want to know. How easy had it been for him to acquire the kind of ID that a legitimate person had to jump through hoops to get?

"Thank you," he said to the rental car clerk as he took the keys, then tilted his head to Iris.

They started walking out of the airport, and the cold hit her. She pulled at her early fall sweater, taking in the cabs and cars parked, unloading, and the busyness of two lanes of one-way traffic driving past, all trying to find a spot to pick up waiting people.

They crossed to the concrete parkade, where the fleet of rentals were, and past the traces of cleared snow and patches of ice. She said nothing, as she could feel how much closer she was to her kids again. It was an ache she hadn't shared with Raymond, because this was the first time she'd been away from her kids, all of them, in forever.

"Here it is," he said, then pressed the fob of a boring brown Malibu. The lights blinked, and he opened the trunk and tossed in the bags before closing it and looking around, back and forth.

She stood there in front of the car, watching as he parked their luggage cart, still looking right and left again.

"Get in," he said as he went to the driver's side, and he had slid behind the wheel and started the car before she'd even fastened her seatbelt.

"You know, you never answered me inside," she said.

He was driving out of the parkade, and as he maneuvered into traffic, she could feel the excitement of Montana, being back home, counting the minutes until she could see her kids. Then there was the baby. If it had been born, she didn't want to miss one moment.

"Best no one knows too much about where we are at any time," he said. "We never know who's listening.

Careful is careful, as I told you before. We need to be vigilant. Even though I'm officially dead, you know it takes just one second of carelessness, someone saying something or questioning things, just one person talking to the wrong person, to blow my cover."

She knew what he was saying and why he was living the life of a man who'd always look over his shoulder. But here she was now, feeling very much an accomplice for the first time. "Okay, I get it."

"Just making sure you do," he said. "Should we go over it again? Who am I?"

The way he said it brought her back to the lessons, the way he'd grilled her while packing about where they'd met, who he was, and how she needed to be careful not to slip.

"You're Jake," she said. "We met at the beachside bar in Barbados, the Blue Fin. I was drinking a lime margarita. You ordered a beer, Corona with lime. You commented on our lime fondness, and we struck up a conversation and a friendship. You're retired—"

"Self-employed," he shot back. "Come on, Iris. You can't mess up on this."

"Right, sorry."

What was it, again? Right, a car wash and fast-food joint under a franchise in California.

"Buddy's Burgers and a car wash down in San Diego," she said. "You're hands-off now, but you check in. Look, I know it's important. I get the name and everything, but do I have to know the business? And why a car wash and fast-food place? Why not just say you're retired? It's easier."

"And it wouldn't work," he said. "People need to imagine me as someone else, and Jake from California, who owns a car wash and fast-food restaurant, is different than Raymond O'Connell, who's supposed to be dead. So come on, remember. This is important because of what we're walking back into. Even though the family is there, I need there to be no questions. You met someone new. He's an entrepreneur. When the identity of that new person is in people's minds, they won't question it when you leave. They'll just assume we're back in California, and you're traveling back and forth between my life and yours."

She took in the icy highway, the heavy clouds that promised more snow. That was one of the things she'd missed out here, the snow, the winter, and the cold, even though it had been nice to spend the time she had with Raymond on a sandy beach in the warm sun. Home was home.

"Yeah, so, about that," she said. "You know this is the first time I've been away from the kids. Seven weeks is a long time. I'm not too anxious to leave again. Can we just settle for a bit and catch our breath?" She clutched her small purse, which was resting on her lap. With her sweater on, at least she was comfortable now in the car, where the heat was blasting.

Raymond said nothing, still wearing the glasses and ballcap, looking out the window and passenger side. For a minute, she didn't think he'd answer, but he did. "You have to have a separate life from the kids. They're grown, and we can't stay here all the time. I have to keep up a front. We can come back, but it's important to keep moving."

She could see the familiar sights of Livingston and felt the urgency of getting home, her home, and being near her kids. She had to talk to them, to see them, to find out if Charlotte had had the baby.

"You're not saying anything, Iris," he said. "This can't be a long visit." Then he glanced her way again, and she took in the O'Connell blue eyes of a man who'd broken her heart so badly that she'd wondered for a long time whether she'd ever be whole again.

"Don't rush me, Raymond."

"Jake." He cut her off. "Start calling me that now. I can't have you slipping."

"Jake, seriously? I want to see the kids, everyone. I want time with my grandchildren, and don't forget you still need to make things right with Brady. You've never talked to him, and the only things you know are what Marcus and Karen have said. He's had only the kids to lean on, to talk to. When this all went down, it was too long before he knew the truth, just like I did, that you weren't dead. I can tell you that thinking you were dead gutted me. What did it do to him? You need to talk to Brady and settle things with him, as well."

Raymond tapped the steering wheel and dragged his hand over the new beard he'd started, a motion she was starting to realize meant he was trying to figure something out. But then she realized he was always thinking, always considering, always planning. "I hear you, Iris, and I will, but as you said, Brady is doing well. He's got Karen and Jack when Luke is gone, and he's with Luke when he's home, and…"

"And I know very well, Raymond O'Connell, a.k.a. Jake," she added quite sharply as she slid around in her seat, seeing how close they were to being home, "that you've been checking in on everyone, all the kids. Where you're getting your information from, I'm not sure I want to know, but I know you haven't shared everything about them. As I said to you, I'm not spying on the kids. I'll call them and ask them. You getting informalion from afar is different than having an actual conversation with them, sitting down with them face to face, so they know you actually care and are part of their lives…"

"I hear you, Iris," Raymond said, cutting her off again. "But remember, for eighteen years, that was the only way I could know what was going on with all of you. It was the only way I could know if there was something wrong, a problem with the kids or with you, so I could handle things and fix them from a distance. So yes, I'll keep spying and checking, because at least I can do that."

She hadn't missed how defensive he sounded. As she glanced out the windshield again, looking straight ahead, seeing downtown, she knew they were only blocks from Owen's old house. She found herself reaching over and resting her hand on Raymond's thigh, patting it, knowing she'd been given the greatest gift, one she'd never thought she'd have: the chance to grow old with the love of her life, who she thought had been taken from her. At least they had that now, in this odd, undercover hiding kind of way.

"Don't be so testy," she said. "And if you don't mind, let's go home first so I can change, and then I'll call Marcus again. Depending on where things stand, we'll have the kids over tonight, and you can sit down and have some one-on-one time with Brady."

He dragged his gaze over to her and then back to the road as he settled his hand over hers. It was his touch, their closeness, that she loved about him. "Fine, but it has to be low key, Iris. Seriously, don't get too comfortable being home, because as soon as you see the kids and meet the baby and be the mother bear you are, making sure they're okay, we'll be leaving again."

Right, on the move, and then what?

Instead of answering, she looked straight ahead and linked her fingers with his. If there was one thing she knew about Raymond O'Connell, it was that he tended to come up with plans and implement them before she had any idea something was in the works, so if he caught on that she wasn't on the same page as him and wouldn't be going along with his plans, he wouldn't stop until he convinced her that his way was the only way.

What he didn't realize was that Iris was smarter than that. Right now, she was seeing her kids, and she had no intention of leaving again until she was good and ready.

CHAPTER
Five

"Careful, come on, watch your step," Marcus said as he helped Charlotte up the steps to their house. As he unlocked the door, taking in how quiet the street was in the early morning, he couldn't remember ever having been so tired, even though he'd pulled a lot of all-nighters before.

The sun was just starting to rise, though thick, heavy clouds hid the light. He glanced across the street to Ryan and Jenny's, seeing a light on in the house and knowing someone was up, but he hoped they wouldn't come running over right now. At the same time, he needed to check on Eva.

"I'm doing the best I can, Marcus, considering I can't see my feet anymore," Charlotte said.

He opened the door and flicked on the light, following her in, seeing how tired she appeared. She had outright refused to stay in the hospital. There had been no labor, but since her water had broken, the doctor had agreed with her that waiting at home, where she'd be more comfortable, was a great idea. She would rest, but for how long? A few hours, maybe. They'd reassess in twenty-four if labor still hadn't started.

He closed the door and reached for Charlotte's coat as she struggled to pull it off, and he tossed it over the curve of the dark wood railing. She sat down on the step and reached down to take off her shoes.

"I'll get that," he said as he squatted down and pulled off her black slip-ons, the only ones now that didn't hurt her feet.

"You've been really quiet since we left the hospital," she said.

He took in her plump face, her full lips. He loved her so much, even though he'd had to fight the urge to wrap his hands around her and shake her when she'd said no to staying in the hospital, since that was all he had wanted her to do.

She could be so damn stubborn.

"What do you want me to say, Charlotte? I would be more comfortable with you staying in the hospital. I said that to the doctor and you, but you both overruled me."

"You heard the doctor. There's no labor," she said, resting her hand on his arm as he pulled off her last shoe and dumped it on the floor. "You also heard her say this sometimes happens, water breaking first, and there's no cause for alarm right now because the baby's heartbeat is strong and everything looks good. She checked me. She's the professional, and she's right: I am more comfortable at home. I'm going to have a shower, go to bed, and get some rest, and when labor starts, then we'll go to the hospital, not before I need to."

She sounded way too calm for a first-time mom. He was having a hard time understanding why he was so rattled. He was a sheriff, after all. He should've been the calm one, not her.

He stood up, and her gaze followed him as he reached out for her hand and pulled her up too, then leaned in and pressed a kiss to her lips before her hand slid over his chest and pushed.

"I know you're angry," she said. "It's just something you can't hide with me. I'm tired, and when labor starts, I kind of want to be rested instead of feeling this bone tiredness I'm feeling right now…"

"And you can't do that in the hospital?" he said.

She was shaking her head as she turned on the stairs and started up, and he dumped his own coat over hers on the railing and followed her, seeing that she was having trouble walking up. He could sense that she wasn't about to concede. She could really dig in and stop listening to any argument he had when she'd made her mind up about something. It was just her personality, something he loved about her, though it frustrated him at times.

"Resting in a hospital? Seriously, Marcus, there's nothing restful about being in the hospital, with the lights and noise and someone coming in constantly and checking on you and poking and prodding just when you drift off, and that's if you fall asleep. No, I want my own bed, our comfortable bed, and a few quiet, undisturbed hours. Besides, I'm hungry, too. If you could make me some toast while I shower… Oh, and could you call Ryan and Jenny and see if they can keep Eva for a while longer? I miss your mom. She was always here for Eva, helping me out. I guess I just secretly wished she'd be here now."

Right, how could he forget? He followed Charlotte into their bedroom, taking in the bed he'd made that morning, or had it been the morning before? "I forgot to mention this in all the excitement, but my mom called last night. That's who I was talking to when your water broke. She's coming back and wanted it to be a surprise. She wants to be here when the baby's born, only I don't think it'll be for a few days yet. She doesn't want me telling anyone, though, so you're the only one in the loop."

He heard the knock downstairs as he took in the way Charlotte's face lit up. She had a beautiful smile even when she was tired. "That's great news," she said. "Okay, I'll shower, and you go answer the door. Who do you think it is?"

He rested his hand on the doorframe as Charlotte pulled off her sweater and tossed it on the bed. His baby would be there anytime, and maybe that was why he was suddenly feeling that this was all too real. "I don't know," he said. "Likely Ryan or Jenny. I'll go talk to them and make you some breakfast."

Marcus strode down the stairs as there was another knock on the door, and he pulled it open to find Ryan dressed in his ranger's uniform, with a heavy coat overtop. Across the street, his pickup was running, evidently warming up from the cold that had settled in. A few flakes of snow were starting to come down.

"You're home," Ryan said. "Jenny said she saw you pull up. What happened?" He stepped in and closed the door behind him.

"No labor," Marcus said. "The doctor said she can rest here at home until it starts, even though I'd prefer her in the hospital."

He started into the kitchen, hearing the shower now going upstairs, and he pulled a loaf of bread from the freezer and rested it on the counter. The coffee pot was clean, and he pulled open the cupboard and took out the coffee and filters, then glanced to his brother, who was standing off to the side, his expression amused, he thought, or maybe it was commiseration.

"So I take it you want us to keep Eva?" Ryan said.

Marcus only nodded as he filled the carafe with water and dumped it in the reservoir, then flicked the switch. "If you could. Charlotte's going to bed and getting some sleep, and I need to check in with Harold and make sure everything's being handled at the office. I may have to stop in, as well. No, I should stop in, but I don't want to leave Charlotte alone. Oh, and I'm not supposed to tell you this, but Mom called last night, and she's on her way back. She wants to surprise everyone, but I told her we've had enough surprises in this family for a lifetime, and I'm not about to keep another secret. Just don't tell Alison or Eva. She really wants to surprise them. And what happened with Brady? I take it Luke took him home."

He wasn't sure what to make of the way his brother glanced away, unsmiling, his jaw set. Okay, something was going on, something he'd missed. Ryan glanced to the door and then back to him before he nodded. "It's great that Mom will be home…"

"I sense a 'but' coming. Something going on with Luke that I should know about?"

There it was again, in his expression, the way his eyes seemed to flash with the kind of untethered anger Marcus had seen in his brother only a few times before.

"You know what?" Ryan said. "You have Charlotte to think about. There's nothing you need to worry about right now. We'll talk after. Tell me, when you say Mom's coming home, does that mean she's alone?"

Marcus braced himself for a talk about their dad, which they had avoided so far. "Nope," he said. "Good old Dad is working out logistics and stuff. She does sound happy, though."

Ryan shrugged, and Marcus wasn't sure what to think. They'd all had their struggle with the Raymond O'Connell situation and the fact that it seemed he was suddenly back in their lives. "Well, good," Ryan said. "She deserves to be happy. Listen, we've got Eva, don't worry. Just wanted to check in, and I would be remiss in not saying that if you want Jenny or Alison here, one can come over this morning. If you need to take off, just call. Alison has the day off today, and Jenny isn't working. Listen, I've got to go. I've got an early meeting, but call Jenny anyway and let us know if labor starts or if you need anything."

Ryan started to the door, and Marcus followed as he opened it and stepped out, then hesitated. The flakes of snow were starting to thicken. "Today will be a fun one, by the looks of it. Think the forecast called for a few inches of snow. I can send Alison over now, you know, seriously."

It wasn't lost on Marcus how Ryan hadn't said anything else about their mom or good old Raymond or Luke and whatever was going on with him.

"I'll call Jenny if I need her," Marcus said. "If you don't mind, could you let everyone know we're home and the baby is taking its time? I don't want a ton of calls filling up my voicemail, which I haven't checked yet."

Ryan laughed. "Yeah, I'll call Suzanne, since she has too much time on her hands, and tell her to ring up everyone and tell them to back off." He started down the steps.

"You know, Ryan, you may as well tell me now what's going on with Luke. Is it something I need to worry about? Because you're about the worst at hiding anything."

Ryan stopped at the bottom step and turned around, seeming to consider it. "You'll likely hear about it later," was all he said, which did nothing to settle anything for Marcus.

"Now you're being cryptic, so if it's all the same to you, I'd rather just hear it now."

Ryan glanced away again, still considering, and then

back to him. "Fair enough," he said. "We met Luke's lady last night, Rosemary."

From the way he said it, Marcus wondered for a moment whether he really did want to hear this. "Yes, I remember, pretty girl. If I recall, that's the first time Luke has brought a woman home to meet us." He could feel a smile tugging at his lips. Had she said something that upset someone, or had there been a disagreement or something?

"Well, what you don't know is who her brother is," Ryan said.

His smile disappeared, and a knot tightened in his stomach. Yeah, maybe he didn't want to know right now, but he said, "I guess you'd better tell me."

"The man who held a gun to Mom and Eva, the one who broke into your house. Ben was his name, right? Well, Rosemary is his sister."

He stared at Ryan for a second. His brother was standing there, waiting as Marcus tried to get his brain on board with what he'd just heard.

God dammit! He was going to seriously hurt Luke.

CHAPTER
Six

She stared at her image in the mirror, the dark circles under her eyes, as she brushed her teeth. Her long hair was a mess, and the light auburn highlights were starting to fade. It was time for another dye job. Maybe she'd go all red, a lighter, brighter shade this time.

Jack leaned against the sink, right beside her, his arms crossed, looking down on her, dressed so casually in a pair of sweats and a T-shirt, and she wondered for a moment whether he'd start in on her again.

Karen spit in the sink, then turned on the tap and filled a cup with water to rinse her mouth. She spat again and rinsed off her toothbrush before tucking it back in the holder beside Jack's. He handed her a towel before she could reach for it, and she hesitated only a second before taking it.

"Thank you," she said.

He didn't smile, just blew out a breath and leaned back against the sink, so close he was almost touching her. She would have to walk around him to leave the bathroom, because he was right there in her space. She squeezed the towel after wiping her face and hands, and he took it from her and ran his hand down her arm, over the gray long-sleeved shirt she wore over cream-colored sweats, something she never slept in but had the night before.

"We need talk to talk about this, and you need to call your doctor," Jack said. It was the same thing he'd hammered into her over and over since getting her into the car at Marcus's, until she'd walked into the bathroom, locked the door, and ran the bath. Then she had just sat there until the water went cold, because she didn't want to talk about the fact that her excitement, terror, and joy had crashed and burned in a matter of seconds.

"Jack, stop. I don't want to talk about this."

"Well, we're going to. You can't just drop a bomb on me like you did last night, saying you were pregnant and then telling me you lost the baby, then giving me the silent treatment. What the hell am I supposed to think, Karen? This isn't the way to handle this. You haven't told me when you found out. I have a hundred questions. I have every right to know."

"You mean like I had the right to know about the governor ticket? Seriously, Jack, how long did you know before you told me? Seems we both have secrets."

Okay, maybe she shouldn't have said it quite like that. A dark expression filled his face, and something flickered in those icy blue eyes. His mouth was set firm amid the whiskers that had turned into a beard, which he'd have to start trimming soon. He stood up slowly, away from the sink, right into her space, and she took a step back from the energy that moved through him. He was furious, pushed too far.

"I didn't mean it like that," she said, lifting her hands to sweep her hair back.

He angled his head and didn't pull his gaze, not

backing down. "The call came yesterday before I picked up Brady," he said. "If you recall, you were in a meeting, and we swung by and picked you up after. I told you as soon as you and I were alone, the first chance I had. I wasn't hiding anything. I wasn't about to talk in front Brady, because this was between you and me. So enough trying to turn this on me, Karen. We're talking about this, the baby, and who's hiding things from who. When, exactly, did you find out you were pregnant and had lost the baby? I have a right to know everything."

The demand in his voice was clear, and she pulled in a breath, trying to figure out how to tell him, to talk about this. She went to take a step around him, because the words just wouldn't come, but his hand slapped around her arm and held her. She could feel his strength even though he wasn't hurting her.

"No, you're not walking away again," he said. "I'm tired of you doing this every time shit hits the fan and you don't want to talk about something. You ignored me all night and then crawled into bed and gave me your back, going to sleep without answering me. Not this morning, Karen…"

She just shook her head and swallowed, feeling tired even though she'd slept. "I just need to settle my head," she said, breathing out, and he dropped his hand as if he were done with her. His mood had gone from confrontational to dismissive, and he walked out of the bathroom, running his hand through his thick dark hair.

She heard him yank open a drawer in the bedroom. The way he did it, she knew he was pissed, and when she stepped out, he had his back to her and was sitting on the unmade bed, pulling on socks.

She pulled her arms across her chest as she leaned in the doorway, just staring at his back even though she could see his face in the mirror of the dresser. "I wasn't sure I was pregnant. I was just feeling tired, not well…off. I hadn't realized I was late. I dropped in to see my doctor two days ago, and she did a blood test and a pregnancy test. I found out then and was just waiting for the official word from the blood test. I was planning on telling you when I knew for sure, but when the doctor called yesterday, she said the blood test showed that although I had been pregnant, the HCG levels meant I had likely miscarried."

Jack slid around on the bed from where he sat and said nothing. His gaze reached out to her. He was quiet, thinking, and she couldn't hide from him when he looked at her the way he was now. "Your first call should've been to me, the moment you knew, the moment you suspected. You aren't in this by yourself. This is you and me, in this together. Why didn't you say anything to me about not feeling well? You had to wonder if you were pregnant. You said the doctor told you you'd likely miscarried, so you don't know for sure? Like, what the hell, Karen? Then you were drowning your sorrows last night at your brother's…"

He was standing now, quickly heading to that place where he was ready to rant and carry on. Maybe he'd even yell at her. He took a step and then made a rude sound as he ran his hand over his hair again, rubbing the top of his head, that motion he made when he was frustrated. He looked at the floor and away and then back to her, jabbing his hand her way.

"Get your shoes on," he said. "Let's go."

"What?" She moved away from the doorway at the demand in his tone. "Go where? Why?"

He walked to the dresser again, really digging in, and yanked open her drawer to pull out socks and toss them to her, hard, fast. She knew he was really pissed as she grabbed them.

"Put those on now," he said. "We're leaving. And call your doctor, or I swear to God I will, Karen. I'm done with this bullshit of yours. Likely miscarried? No, we're dealing with this right now, and if your doctor won't see us, we're going to the hospital. You don't get to slip into silence and not share anything. You seem to forget this is my baby, too. If you're pregnant, I should know the moment you do, the moment you think you are. The moment you weren't feeling well, the moment you called the doctor, you should have said something, yet you said nothing. Two days ago, really?"

Karen just pulled in a breath and then another as she clutched the socks, feeling the bite of his words. She didn't want to have to deal with his ego or his frustration. She tossed the socks on the bed and then strode out of the bedroom, taking in the open door to her home office, with its daybed, where Brady had slept, his clothes on the floor and the bed unmade.

She picked up the clothes and thought she heard Jack swear under his breath. Yeah, she had the ability to push all his buttons and provoke him. She just couldn't help it. She dumped Brady's black jeans in the wicker hamper in the corner along with his shirts and socks and T-shirts and the pants he slept in, then started to make the daybed, pulling up the sheets and the comforter. She reached for the pillow on the floor when she heard Jack behind her, and she turned to see him in the doorway, unsmiling, dragging his hand over his face with a scrape of whiskers.

"Karen, put your shoes on, please."

It was the calmness in his tone that had her holding the pillow against her stomach, against her chest. She stood there and took in the man she loved so deeply, who had turned her life upside down and likely always would.

Everything about them together was anything but easy. He took another step, a rather calm one, toward her.

"Please, for once, just do as you're told," he said. "Make it easy and stop fighting me." His voice was soft and low, and he pulled in another breath as he strode toward her and reached for the pillow she was holding so tightly. He gave it a gentle tug and pulled it from her hands, then tossed it on the bed.

The way he touched her and slid his hand over her arm, the way he pulled her gently toward him, a step closer, she felt her eyes burn, felt her throat thicken. He pulled her against him, his hand sliding over the back of her head as she fisted his shirt, and she couldn't fight the tears, though she didn't understand where they'd come from.

"Shh…" was all he said as she cried against him. He pressed a kiss to the side of her head as he held her so tightly. "Why do you have to make everything a fight?" He kissed her head again, holding her so close, just letting her cry.

CHAPTER
Seven

"So you still haven't told me how it was, staying with Karen and Jack," Luke said. "And you haven't filled me in on school, girls, any problems you've had—or whatever has you staring endlessly at that phone."

He took in the sun rising above the horizon through the kitchen window as the coffee finished brewing. Brady was wearing sweats and a T-shirt, his hair sticking up, as he worked on his second bowl of cereal. He had taken the last of the Oaty-O's, which were also Luke's favorite.

Brady put down his cell phone and shoved another huge bite of cereal in his mouth, then just stared in that stubborn way of his, chewing, maybe deciding what not to say. He shoved over the carton of milk, which was also empty, sitting on the counter beside him. Evidently, a trip to the grocery store was in order, considering his mom was gone and nothing had been stocked and waiting for him when he came home.

"She still sleeping?" was Brady's only response. He stared into his bowl from where he sat at the island, on a stool, slouched over, teenage, tall, and lanky, before flicking his eyes up to Luke again. Even though Brady was his brother, he was the only one in the family without the O'Connell blue eyes.

"Who, Rosemary?" Luke said. He glanced toward the hall, picturing Rosemary where he'd left her, sound asleep in his bed. "Yeah, she's not a morning person. You didn't answer me. We're talking about you and how you're doing, so don't change the subject."

"Well, what about you changing the subject? Is she really who Ryan and Owen said, and is her brother? Did he really try to hurt Iris and Eva?"

What was he supposed to say? He'd never believed his family would understand, and maybe that was why he'd never brought her around until the night before. He'd tried to tell himself over and over that it was a bad idea, getting involved with her.

Sex had been just sex—until it wasn't.

"Yes, it was her brother who broke into Marcus's, but he was after me. It was because of me, to get to me over something I'd done to his family. It put my mom and Eva in the line of fire. But if everyone in my family wants to be angry with someone, they should really be angry with me, considering I was the one who brought my work home, back here.

"You don't have your head buried in the sand, kid. You know what I do. You know what your dad did, too, and the kind of people we deal with. I have a team, and we do the kinds of things that make a lot of enemies. You also saw what went down that night at your old house, you and Alison. We don't live in a world of fairytales and butterflies. Rosemary was caught in the middle, too. Is she responsible in any way for what happened? No. So stop changing the subject, and let's talk about you and how you're doing. I noticed something was up with my sister and Jack, too. You know what that's about?"

Brady dumped his spoon back in the bowl with a clatter and pushed it away, then shrugged as he finished chewing. There was a lot Brady just wouldn't talk about, including the night he thought he'd watched his dad die, when he'd had a gun in his face and been tied up and terrorized. No one could walk out of that without some kind of battle scars. Luke wondered now why Brady didn't hate him for having to lie the way he had, telling him Raymond was dead.

"I don't know," Brady said. "Jack and Karen are always working on something, a case. They never seem to agree. Well, no. Rather, Karen never agrees with whatever Jack says. I swear, she disagrees with him just because it was his idea. Then they do this big back-and-forth—and, by the way, Karen isn't quiet. Jack starts out quiet but gets louder, and I can see how she provokes him. To tell you the truth, I think she really enjoys it, but I don't think he has any idea what she's doing and how she does it.

"They're always in my business, asking about school, what I'm thinking, what I'm doing. They argue all the time, and when I said something to Karen about it, she said they don't argue; they discuss and disagree and verbally spar. I pointed out to her that it sounded like arguing, and I also told her I think she enjoys it too much. She just smiled. Jack gets off on it, too, though, I think. Karen is so stubborn. She doesn't let anything go. I find it easier not to say anything when she's talking about something, or I just agree when she gets in my face. And now she's doing my laundry, too. You have to tell her to stop." Brady was sitting up straighter. Luke could see that his sister was getting under his skin.

Luke rested his hand on the counter and leaned back

as he reached for the carafe of coffee as soon as it had filled enough, then poured it in the "My Favorite Son" mug, which he used every time he was there. It was his mug, the only one he ever wanted to drink from.

He slid his gaze over to Brady and watched as he lifted his glass of orange juice and downed the rest, knowing he didn't drink coffee. "If you've picked up on anything about my sister, then you know you don't tell Karen to stop anything. She's going to do what she sets her mind to, and no one can convince her of anything until she's good and ready. She wants to pick up after you, then you tell her to stop. You're a big boy. Use your words with her, but I can't guarantee she'll listen.

"You're her shiny new toy, you know. When Dad left, it hit Karen harder than anyone. She took it out on our mom, and she wasn't nice about it. She was Dad's favorite. We all knew it. Her getting her hands on you and not letting anyone else have you is just her way of dealing with the dad issue, though she'll never admit it."

Brady frowned. It was clear he still had a lot to learn about his sister, about all of them. Maybe Luke would call Karen later, maybe ask her to stop by, have a talk face to face about what was going on with her and Jack, then give her the spiel about dialing back her over-mothering of Brady. Then there was Rosemary. What was he going to do about her?

"So, girls, school?" he continued. "Come on, spill. There has to be something else."

Brady set down his empty glass and stared at Luke with that mutinous gaze that let him know he wasn't getting anything else.

"You know I have other ways of finding out," Luke said. As Brady stepped off the stool, he could see he had grown, and he thought for a second that his little brother might have an inch on him now.

"Well, then knock yourself out," Brady said. "As I told Karen and Jack in the car yesterday, school's done for me. I have everything I need to graduate, and I'm not wasting another minute on any useless classes I don't need. So I'm going to look for a job, something I've never had but always wanted. Now, at least Dad isn't dragging me around the world before I can get settled anywhere, make friends, get a job, do the kinds of things normal people do. For the first time, I want to find something. I don't care what it is, but I'm going to get a job. As for girls, well, I'm not dating or seeing anyone, and if I was, I wouldn't tell you. Problems? Who doesn't have any, especially considering who our father is? Anything else?"

Luke lifted his mug and took a swallow of coffee as he narrowed his gaze, expecting Brady to walk out. "Yeah, you asked about Rosemary," he said. "Well, just so you know, while she's here, treat her with respect, okay? Don't jump right to judge, jury, and executioner because of what Owen and Ryan said. She's nice, and I like her—a lot. She's not her brother, and if you want to get into the nitty-gritty of it, if any of you knew even a few of the things I've done for this country, I'm pretty sure you would never want to speak with me again."

He knew he sounded like an asshole, but if someone had done to his family what he and his team had done to Rosemary's father, he'd likely have taken the same path as her brother.

Brady stared long and hard at Luke. "Fine, but what about Marcus, Suzanne, and Karen, when they find out? Have you thought of that?"

He heard the floor squeak and took in Rosemary as she

stepped into the kitchen, wearing a robe of his that he never wore, her hair a mess. He wondered how close she was to packing and running out the door.

"Yeah, Luke, that's a great question," she said. "Good morning, Brady." She strode in, seeing the coffeemaker and opening the cupboard to pull out a mug as if she knew where everything was. She poured herself a coffee before turning around in the silence, and Luke realized they were both waiting for him to say something.

"I'll talk to them," he said. "But they don't know the whole story…"

That was all he got out before he heard a car door, then footsteps, then a key in the lock. The front door opened, which had him stepping out of the kitchen and into the hallway, where he saw his mom and Raymond.

Holy shit!

"What are you doing here?" he said. "Thought you were enjoying the sun and sand."

Raymond closed the door. He wore glasses and a ball-cap, with the start of a beard. Iris kicked off her shoes, wearing a sweater that would've done nothing against the chill outside.

"Not when Charlotte is about to have the baby," she said. "I wanted to be here, so here we are. It's great to see you. Have you heard anything this morning from Marcus?"

He just shook his head, glancing over his shoulder to Brady, who had an odd look on his face as his mom and dad started into the kitchen. Luke took in the panic he hadn't seen before from Rosemary, and he moved over to her, next to Brady, who was now leaning on the counter in silence. Luke wasn't sure how to tackle this, and now, he was thinking she had been right about not coming over.

"Heard nothing yet," he said. "We just got up, so we

haven't had a chance to call anyone. Besides, I'm sure Marcus will call and give us an update. Don't babies take a while?"

His mom stood there, staring at Rosemary with a smile. He wondered whether it would still be there when she learned who she was. Raymond was right behind her, and just one look told Luke that his dad did know.

"This is Rosemary," he said. He would've reached for her hand, but the way she stood, holding the coffee mug, her other wrapped across her waist, he knew she wasn't about to make this easy. She'd gone into that defensive mode, as if getting ready for another attack. At this point, more questions might be the final straw for her. "But before you get all happy, Mom, she already took a shit-kicking from Ryan and Owen, so if there are any more questions from anyone, I'll say thanks, but if it's all the same, we'll be leaving."

His mom was confused, but Raymond rested his hands on her shoulders, offered a smile to Rosemary, and said, "Rosemary, I heard a lot about you from Luke. Glad you could come, and it's nice to meet you. Luke, we need to talk. Brady…"

Brady, who was standing with his arms crossed, turned to Luke as if he hadn't heard his dad and said, "I'm taking the shower first." Then he walked out of the kitchen, giving his dad a wide berth.

"I guess I need to talk to him," Luke said.

Iris hadn't pulled her gaze from Rosemary, and she pulled in a sharp breath. "Why would Ryan and Owen be upset with Rosemary? Did something happen? I think you should fill me in." She dragged her gaze from Raymond over to Luke, who took in the way Rosemary stared down into her coffee, lost, angry, uncomfortable—likely all three.

"Because her brother was Ben Schwartz," Luke said. "The Ben Schwartz who—"

"Who broke into Marcus's place, terrorized me and Eva, held a gun to my head, and would have killed us," his mom said, cutting him off. Her voice had risen, maybe from shock, a tone that was usually followed by a tongue-lashing of some kind. He wasn't sure what to do next, and she breathed out in a way he hadn't heard before.

"I see," she said, then pressed her hands together and dropped them. "But that wasn't you, Rosemary. Well, you know what? We've been flying all night to get home. I haven't slept. I need a shower, and then I'm going to call Marcus and find out about Charlotte, how she is, and where my grandbaby is."

The smile on his mom's face was forced. He could see that as she dragged her gaze over to him and then back to Rosemary before saying, "Okay then. Well, sorry about this. Rosemary, it's nice to meet you."

Then she was gone, and that left Rosemary and Luke and his dad, who pulled off his glasses and rested them on the counter. Luke didn't miss the puzzled expression on Rosemary's face when he did.

"Luke, can I have a word with you?" Raymond said.

Rosemary rested her mug on the counter. "You know what? I'm going to…uh, leave you two." She gestured to the living room, and he could see how rattled she was as she stepped out.

"So I see you listened to me," Raymond said, watching Rosemary walk out before looking over to Luke with an expression he wasn't entirely sure about.

"I did, but as with some things, Pops, I'm thinking it may not have been the smartest thing I've done."

His dad said nothing as he looked back down the hall. What he was staring at or thinking, Luke didn't know.

"Well, I guess only you can decide that, considering the sneaking around you've been doing. You either keep doing that or come clean, but if you thought it was going to be easy, you should've known better." He rested his hand on Luke's shoulder. "And as I know better than anyone, you just need to give everyone some time. Let them get to know her. Is she anything like her brother?"

"No," Luke said, biting the word out. "She's not her brother."

His dad smiled and inclined his head before stepping back. "Well, then everyone will know that. You just need to tell your siblings, and they'll come around. I'm going to go join your mom. She wants to see all her kids. Oh, and just so you know, because I can't really exist, my name's Jake Peters now. I'm from California, but we'll talk about my cover later. And, uh…" He glanced down the hall again before looking back over to Luke. "How you feel about Rosemary is all that matters. Give everyone time to get to know her. They'll come around. I've seen you all together. Or you could go back to living how you think everyone expects you to, sneaking around, but that isn't going to make anyone happy, especially you."

"So what do you expect me to do?"

His dad smiled. "I expect you to find a way to figure it out. There's always a way. If she makes you happy, then you find a way to get everyone to see that she isn't her brother, just like your family isn't responsible for what you do, what I do, what we've done."

Raymond let his meaning sink in, then walked away, and Luke heard him tap on the bathroom door, where Brady was currently using up the hot water. "Hey, there's a houseful here who needs the shower! Shut it down," he called out.

That left Luke alone in the kitchen, knowing the easiest

course of action would be to drive Rosemary home and say goodbye. But then, in everything he did and had done, he had never taken the easy way.

CHAPTER
Eight

"I won't be gone long," Marcus said to Alison. "Charlotte is upstairs, sleeping, so let her sleep. I'm not too keen about leaving, but I have to stop in and take care of a few things."

Marcus was still bothered by the call from Harold. After a late-night emergency city council meeting, they had been ordered to handle some campers in the park. It wasn't something he could pass off to his deputy.

He took in his niece, who wore a baggy sweatshirt and sweats, as well as a nose ring he hadn't noticed the night before. Her dark hair was shoulder length, and her feet were bare, but at least she'd worn boots to trudge across the street, coatless, after Jenny put Eva in the back of her Jeep to take her to school.

"Sure, I can do that," Alison said, pulling out the earbuds plugged into her cell phone, which she tucked into the front pocket of her baggy sweatshirt.

"So you're off school today?" Marcus said.

Alison shrugged. "I'm done my homework and caught up. I don't need to be there today."

Whatever that was supposed to mean, he wasn't sure. He took her in, waiting for her to add anything else, but this was Alison, and depending on her mood, she was either chatty or not.

"Right, okay," he said. "So your mom took Eva to school, and I shouldn't be long, but do me a favor. If you're listening to music, keep it down so you can keep an ear out for Charlotte. Food's in the fridge, so help yourself to anything, and call me if anything comes up." He held up his cell phone as if to make a point, to be sure she understood, as he pulled on his heavier coat and pocketed his phone. "If there's anything, I mean anything, you call me."

"Yeah, sure. Don't wake Charlotte, and don't listen to music. I'll just sit here, staring at the wall."

For a second, he wondered if his expression showed his alarm.

"Just kidding, Uncle Marcus. You should see your face! I got this."

"Right," was all he managed to get out.

He glanced once up the stairs and then said nothing else as he stepped outside into the cold. The snow was falling, not heavy, just enough that he knew the roads would likely become a problem later. He thought of the emergency he had to deal with, and it had to be dealt with today, this morning, an order from the council. There were just some things about his job that he didn't like.

He brushed off the snow that had already fallen on the sheriff's car, which he'd started earlier, so it was now warm as he climbed behind the wheel. He pulled out just as his cell phone rang from where it was settled in the dash mount. He pressed the green answer button.

"Harold, on my way," he said. "Give me ten minutes."

"Change of plans," Harold said. "Ryan called. He's already there, and so is Lonnie."

"Why is Lonnie there? I told you to make sure he stays in the office. I don't want him out there, stirring things up."

"Well, appears someone on the council is still calling Lonnie to handle things. Three guesses who."

He swore under his breath, tired, giving way to the short fuse he was well aware he'd be functioning on today. "Let me guess: Murray Conway, the one who's been vocal about getting me out as sheriff."

There was silence for a second on the other end. "Didn't know you'd heard about that," Harold replied, an edge in his tone.

"I hear everything," Marcus said. "Meet you out there."

He disconnected the phone and flicked on his siren to move cars aside so he could get past as he drove into a neighborhood just outside downtown. He spotted his brother's park ranger truck and two sheriff's vehicles already there. The road was getting slick, and snow was coming down as he took in the park, which was filled with tents and tarps, some being taken down.

Marcus zipped up his coat as he stepped out of his car, seeing a sign on the fence about some development, something else on the county books. He didn't understand why camping had suddenly become a crime for him to handle. Harold wore a knit hat, and Marcus rubbed his bare hands in the cold and walked over to him.

"Seems I missed something," he said. "What happened?"

"Emergency meeting was called late last night. Apparently, some residents in the area complained about the campers not packing up and leaving in the morning. There've been a number of complaints of crime, drugs, garbage being scattered, a couple sheds being broken into, and public urination—because there are no bathrooms, so where the hell else are they supposed to go? A few of the residents have complained that they don't want their parks used as toilets, and we've been ordered by the council to enforce the new bylaw. They can't camp or stay here at all. Everyone who doesn't pack up and leave, we're to arrest them. Oh, and they added that the developer needs to have his equipment in here to start digging, because they're putting in a new condo development, only I don't think the residents in the area know that part."

Marcus stopped walking as he reached into his pocket, pulled out his gloves, and pulled them on, taking in what he thought were maybe twenty tents. All he could do as he took in the sight was think of his Eva and her mother, Reine, because they'd been there, living just like this. It still lingered in the back of his mind, how dire it had been for them.

"I really fucking hate this job sometimes," he said. "So the neighbors complained, but we're really doing this for the developer. So where are we supposed to move them to?"

Harold was walking beside him. It was too damn cold for them to be out here, anyway, he thought, as he took in the houses across the street. Seeing smoke from some of the chimneys, he couldn't help thinking of the warm, comfortable beds everyone in those houses had.

"I already called the homeless warming shelter here, but they're out of beds, and people have to be out during the day," Harold said. "I've put a call in to two of the churches, as well, to see if they can do something. Council gave no solutions about what to do with them, just told us to kick them out."

Ryan was talking to a group, writing something down, and he could see tents being disassembled. Lonnie was putting out someone's fire, and Colby was having a discussion with an old woman. An old man was sitting on a box nearby, with an old coat on, a worn hat that had seen better days. His face was dirty. He saw men, women, a few kids, bundled up in the kinds of clothes people tossed out.

As he walked into the middle of the camp with Harold, he knew everyone was looking his way, and nothing about this left him feeling good.

"Any suggestions would be nice, Marcus," Harold said. "I know you've got a lot on your plate, but it's cold out here, and it's not just frostbite and exposure we need to worry about. These people are tired and have nothing. We can kick them out, but they're going to have to find another spot to rest their heads—or are we supposed to follow them and keep moving them out? It's not a solution. Heard there were some reports of theft, too. Someone's camp stove is missing, and a backpack, money, food. I don't know how people ever end up here."

He stopped with Harold at a small green dome tent, which a man was taking down. He had to be Marcus's age, early thirties, maybe, with light tangled hair sticking out from under his worn, dirty hat, and an old coat, with bare hands. A woman was there, too, rolling up a sleeping bag and blankets, packing up.

"Hey, there," Marcus said. "You folks have a place to go?"

The man tossed a glance over his shoulder, then said to a boy, maybe ten or twelve, "John, finish rolling the tent." Then he turned to Marcus. "No, Sheriff. We were in Bozeman before but were told to move on, so we found this place. I have my wife and two boys. We're on foot now. My pickup was impounded in Missoula along with the tools I stored in the back. I used to work in construction until I was laid off, and I couldn't afford to pay the fine. Was hoping to find some work, but the shelters are full, and now we have to move again. No idea where. Any ideas where I can get something for my kids, my wife? They're cold."

What the hell was he supposed to say? He took in the neighborhood around them. His family had a house and had never been forced, no matter how dire their situation, to live like this. He found himself looking to Harold.

"We're looking for you," Harold said. "I have some calls out…"

"Terrance, my watch is gone," the woman called out, rummaging through a backpack.

The man strode over to her. "Are you sure? It can't be."

Marcus just took in the scene and the bleakness.

Some distance away, Lonnie was in an argument with a man, and suddenly he had him cuffed and on the ground. Marcus strode over just in time to see Lonnie with a knee in the man's back.

"Get off him! He didn't do anything," a guy yelled out.

Marcus wasn't liking this spike in emotions. He'd tried to fire Lonnie, but the council had blocked it. When tempers flared, he didn't want to be on the wrong side of a problem.

"What's going on here?" he called out, stepping in. "Get off him, Lonnie."

"I did nothing wrong," the handcuffed man said as Lonnie yanked him off the ground hard. He had a long scar on his face and smelled bad, with a beard and dark eyes. "He was tossing my things around. I told him to take his hands off them, but he started searching my bags, asking about drugs…"

"So you cuffed him?" Marcus said, giving everything to Lonnie, who was staring back at him with a look he knew well.

Their relationship had broken down to barely tolerating one another, with no respect and a mutual hatred that was significantly deteriorating into something that bordered on insubordination from Lonnie, who was likely undermining him every step of the way. Trust was trust, and there was none between them.

"For safety," Lonnie said. "And I had probable cause for the search. A few over there said he's been dealing in the camp."

Right, of course, was all Marcus could think. "This true? You been dealing drugs?"

The man shook his head. "Who told you that? It's a damn lie," he yelled.

Marcus was aware that the people around them, all packing up, were looking over and watching. From the energy, he could feel that he was seen as the enemy.

"Just sit down on the ground here," Marcus said, taking the man's arm. He sat him down and gestured to Lonnie to move over, crossing his arms. "Someone told you he was dealing drugs. Who?"

Lonnie, who had been a thorn in his side and whom he had no respect for, made a noise and then gestured. "Some of the people who live across the way said drugs have been dealt out here. Crime is up. That's why the council called an emergency meeting. The residents here have been demanding it be cleaned up. They want to come in here with their kids, but look at this mess. There's shit every-where. They step out of their tents and use the bathroom right in front. It's disgusting. Who's going to clean this up? It's an environmental hazard. And you know darn well that criminals hide out in homeless camps."

He just took in Lonnie, then looked down to the man on the ground, sitting there. "You find anything in his bag?"

Lonnie seemed to consider something for a second,

then shook his head. "Nope, but I haven't searched him yet, and I didn't finish looking through his things."

"I've heard nothing that gave you any justification for a search, Lonnie. Uncuff him and let him go. You stay out of his things."

"Marcus, I'm telling you, he's got something…"

"Yeah, well, I'm telling you that when someone actually comes forward with some real evidence that gives probable cause, that's a different story. Instead of being such a goddamn asshole, how about showing some empathy here and offering a solution? You know damn well the only thing the council said was to get these people out of the park. And are we doing it for the residents or the developer?"

Lonnie had backed up, saying nothing, and made no move to uncuff the man.

"Right, so this is how you're playing it," Marcus muttered, then pulled a key from his pocket and gave another glance to Lonnie as he uncuffed the man. He turned to see his brother coming his way, while Harold was still talking to Terrance and his wife and two boys.

"Pack up your things and move on out of here," was all Marcus said to the man. Then he took another step toward Lonnie. "You're not here to harass anyone or search their things. I don't know what you were told to do or handle and for whom, but don't forget you still work for me and report to me."

Before Lonnie could add anything, Marcus walked away.

Ryan was almost to him. "Hey, how's Charlotte? Didn't think you'd be out here," he said.

Marcus couldn't help but see the scattered garbage and the helplessness of the situation. Yeah, someone was going to have to clean this up. "Had no choice, considering this…" He gestured and shook his head.

Ryan's expression was grim too. "Heard the shelter's full already. It's pretty bad here. Talked to a few who are packing up. They said crime's been bad. People are stealing. Seems the criminals and crooks hide out in here. One old woman—she looks eighty, I swear, but she's only in her fifties—said her money was stolen from the socks she stashed it in. If you're a woman on the streets and anyone knows you have money, it's bad for you. Looks like she's got a shiner. Someone knocked her around a bit. I asked her to talk to you, but she's not interested."

He just shook his head, seeing a few already walking with backpacks, full with the weight of what they had.

"How do you think people ever let things get this bad, having nothing?" Ryan asked.

Marcus wondered how to answer. "Oh, I don't know. I suppose once you hit the streets, there is no safety net. I guess we're lucky. Because we have each other, this would never happen to us." He looked over the young family and the way the father was herding his kids. The boys had bags lifted, carrying backpacks. "Owen still has his place empty?"

Ryan just narrowed his gaze. "Since he's living with Tessa, yeah. He keeps it and uses his garage for his plumbing storage and office. Told him to list it, but you know Owen. Why?"

Marcus dragged his gaze over to the young father again, who lifted a backpack with the tent and bags. The gear seemed almost too much for them all to carry. "Because he's got an empty house, and it's cold out." He reached over and smacked his hand over Ryan's chest, then moved toward the family. "Terrance, hold up!" he called.

The man stopped and looked at him, and it was the

look in his eyes that got to Marcus. There was no male ego. He'd had the shit kicked out of him. He said nothing to Marcus, just looked over to his wife and kids, who were bundled in layers. "Yes, Sheriff, what is it?" He sounded tired and pissed.

"Where are you heading?" Marcus said.

The man hesitated a second, wary. "Toward the shelter. Maybe something will open up. Maybe I can get my wife and kids in, at least. But I'm not too interested in saying much else."

Right, so he figured the police would follow them and tell them to move on again. Marcus wondered how many times that had happened.

"I may have something," he said. "Just let me make a call. It's at least a roof, something for now, until you can find your feet."

He wasn't sure, but he swore he saw a mist in the man's eyes, which wasn't from the cold. "I'd appreciate it, Sheriff. I really would."

Marcus only nodded, then pulled out his phone, pulled off his gloves, and turned away.

Harold stepped up to him and said, "What are you doing?"

Marcus dialed Owen's number. "Coming up with a solution for at least one family here. Get Lonnie and Colby to help you find something for everyone here, because this isn't solving a problem, just moving it into someone else's backyard. Call the rec center, all the churches…" He put the phone to his ear as it rang and took in Harold's expression.

"Okay," was all Harold said before walking over to Colby.

"She had the baby?" was how Owen answered.

"Not yet," Marcus said. "But I need you to do something for me, and it's a big ask."

His brother hesitated on the other end. "Fine, sure. What do you need?"

He wondered if Owen would still be saying that when he heard what he was going to ask. "Your house, the empty one that you don't live in… There's a family here that's got no place to go."

There was silence.

"Owen, you there?"

"What, exactly, are you asking me?"

"They just need a roof over their heads. They've had a run of bad luck."

Silence again for another second. "You asking me to rent my house to some strangers? Are you crazy?"

Marcus pulled in a breath, already hearing the no in his brother's voice. "Well, not rent, considering they've got nothing, and I doubt they could pay you anything right now. Just come down here to the park we're being forced to clear out. The homeless are camping here, and there's a lot of people. It's a family who've lost everything, from the looks of it. Just talk to them…but remember Reine and Eva? How about you do the right thing?"

He heard his brother swear on the other end as he waited. "No promises, Marcus. I don't want my house wrecked."

"That's quite a leap, Owen."

"Well, you hear the stories out there."

"You hear one story, and it's not everyone, and it's not the whole story. Don't start profiling, Owen. You know better. We lived through it."

He waited a second, knowing this was a big ask, a big gamble.

"Fine," was all his brother said before he hung up, promising he'd be there soon.

As Marcus stood in the middle of what was left of the camp, seeing the garbage and rot and filth, he wondered how the council could just vote to move them out without offering a solution to a very real problem. But then, there was no money in fixing homelessness, and it seemed no one had the motivation or interest to do the right thing.

Raymond was just getting out of the shower as Iris finished drying her hair. She knew that just on the other side of the closed bedroom door was a woman whose brother had thought nothing of pointing a gun at Eva, at her, and would have killed them without blinking an eye.

She remembered the look in his eyes, the same look she'd seen in the eyes of the man she'd shoved a knife into eighteen years ago.

"I can see you're having some trouble with Rosemary, Iris," Raymond said. "You may have put up a good front, but I know you well. You have something on your mind, so you should say it."

She watched as he dried himself off and hung up the towel after running it over his short dark hair, which was starting to lighten. He strode into her bedroom, their bedroom, and rummaged through his bag of clothes on the bed. He pulled on socks and underwear, then stepped into a clean pair of jeans.

She stood there in her own blue jeans and long-sleeved

white shirt, more for comfort than style. She wanted to check in with Marcus and talk to all her kids, her grandkids. Even though she could use some sleep, she wasn't tired right now. She missed her kids and wanted to see them, and then there was the baby she'd eagerly waited to meet.

"What do you want me to say?" she replied. "I can't believe Luke is involved with a woman whose brother tried to hurt us. No, he had every intention of hurting us and would've killed me if Luke hadn't killed him first."

"Did Rosemary try to hurt you or have a gun on you?" Raymond said, so matter of fact.

"No." She stepped closer to the bed, running her hand over Raymond's back.

He pulled out a maroon long-sleeved knit and pulled it over his head. "Then there's your answer. She didn't do it, so don't go and put what her brother did on her. You can't blame someone for what someone in her family did. If that started happening, then our kids would have a lot of people angry at them."

Something about the way he said it had her hesitating. "Sounds like you know more about Rosemary than I do. How?"

He didn't nod but looked across the room and pulled in a breath before sliding those bold O'Connell blues her way. "You think Luke wasn't conflicted? He never planned to bring her here, because of who her brother is. Yeah, you're right that I knew, and I told Luke to knock it off. He was sneaking around, but he really likes her, and you should know, if you don't already, that the entire situation was complicated and arose out of a gray area. Luke was ordered to do something in the name of national security, and it caused Ben Schwartz to look for payback. Pretty sure Ben, who was holding the gun, is dead now, am I right? Luke killed him. It wasn't Rosemary. Do you really think Luke would bring her around if she had any part in hurting his family? Yeah, I knew pretty much everything about the kids. Had my ways of finding out so that if I had to do something, I could."

Why did he have to put it like that?

She pulled in a breath and then let it out. "It's not always that simple, Raymond," she said, and the way he looked at her had her lifting her hands. "I'm not calling you Jake in private. Then there's the kids."

He stepped closer and lifted his hands to her chin, then leaned in and kissed her. "It is that simple. Do it in private so you don't slip in public. We're talking about giving Rosemary a break, setting an example for the kids." He ran his thumb over her chin and then stepped back. "You should call Marcus and find out about Charlotte and whether the baby is here yet. I'll call Karen and Suzanne, and we'll have everyone over here tonight," he said, already at the bedroom door, pulling it open.

She could hear voices from the kitchen and living room, she thought, as she followed him and said, "You need to sit down with Brady before we see anyone."

There it was, the hesitation. He rolled his shoulders. "Yeah, and then you need to get to know Rosemary. Again, Iris, if Luke's bringing her home…"

"I know, I know. It's serious," she said, cutting him off.

She followed the man she loved as he strode into the living room, where the TV was on, Luke parked on the sofa. In the kitchen, Brady was making a sandwich and staring into the living room, where his dad was. The way he watched him, Iris knew this wasn't just going to be a simple talk, after which everything would be fixed. It was going to be a lengthy process of working through a lot of anger.

IRIS'S FACE lit up when she talked to her kids, Raymond noticed. They'd only just found out that Charlotte was home asleep, Alison with her, as Marcus had been called out to handle some crisis. She was on the phone with Suzanne now, he thought. When he called Karen, it had gone right to voicemail. Luke, he knew, was in his bedroom, convincing Rosemary to stay, and Brady was in the kitchen, where Iris was, eating a sandwich and doing his best to ignore his father.

Well, he supposed biting the bullet, so to speak, was the only way to resolve the Brady problem, so he strode into the kitchen.

Iris was running water at the sink while talking on the phone. Raymond walked right over beside Brady, who was sitting at the island, and leaned over, taking in his son, who was pretending that sandwich he was eating held all the answers.

"How you been, son?" he said, then wondered how long he'd have to wait until Brady relented and looked his way. He counted in his head: One, two…

There it was. He flicked his eyes, so different from those of his siblings, over to him, and Raymond could see the one thing he knew he was trying to hide, the hurt Raymond seemed to leave in his wake among all his kids.

"Fine," Brady said. "Excuse me." He went to slide off the stool and walk away, so Raymond slid his hand over his arm and held it.

"Not so fast," he said. "I want to talk to you."

He realized Iris had turned the water off. She walked around the counter and pressed her hand to Brady's shoulder, the phone still to her ear. "Go talk to your dad in the living room," she said in a way that left no room for discussion.

So what did Brady do but slide off the stool and obey? Iris gave him one of those looks. She seemed to have a knack for talking to Brady in a way Raymond couldn't. She gestured for him to go, so he followed his son into the living room, where he was now sitting on the sofa, slouched as if he were only there because he had been told to be. Which he was.

"I guess the only place to start is to say I'm sorry," Raymond said.

Brady flicked his gaze up to him with not an ounce of give. "Great. Can I go now?"

How had he ever figured this was going to be easy? "No, Brady, you can't. We need to talk. There was no other way. You had to believe I was dead, and so did Iris, and I'm so sorry for that, but it was the only way, or it would never end. The kind of people who were watching are always watching. You have no idea what that did to me, seeing you and Alison tied up like that, knowing very well that those men would never have let you live. It was a bad situation, and I'm sorry I put you through that."

There, he'd said his piece.

But all Brady did was stare at him. "Luke explained everything to me, so I get it. If that's what you're wanting forgiveness for, then sure," he said and stood up, and Raymond just took in the young arrogance looking down at him.

"No, sit down," he said, then gestured, knowing how sharply it had come out. "It's not okay. I need you to sit down and talk. Don't confuse my apology for anything but that. You don't get to dismiss me, Brady. I told you to sit down." He jabbed his hand to the sofa and waited another second, then another, before Brady relented and sat. He could see that he was just a moment away from walking out, though. "You're angry with me, and I get it…"

"Do you really, Dad?" Sarcasm dripped in his tone.

"I do, but I'm not about to walk on eggshells around you in this house. We're a family…"

"You mean the secret family you had, the one you couldn't be bothered to tell me about before sneaking us back into Livingston? You didn't tell me I had brothers and sisters—and then there was Alison. You know how shitty I feel, how she feels? It's so damn awkward now. My hands were on her… I didn't know we were family. You lied to me. Then there's my mom. What was she to you? You left your family, Iris, just abandoned them…" He stopped talking and let out a rude noise. "You know what, Dad? You're forgiven, if that's what you want to hear. I'm a big boy, and I'm getting along fine, but if it's all the same to you, considering I doubt you'll be here long, we can't ever get back to the way it was. We'll never be there again, ever."

Okay, that was a start.

"You're right," Raymond said. "I'm a shithead and an asshole, but when I left Iris and my kids, I didn't do it by choice. Did I love your mother, Nancy? No, I'm sorry. We didn't have that type of relationship. I didn't know about you until she was killed, but I can tell you that I love you very much. Iris is the love of my life. I never thought I'd have her again, and I never expected to have my other kids back in my life with you. I don't expect you to understand everything, Brady, but there are things I did, complicated things…"

Brady leaned his head back and actually rolled his eyes. "Yeah, I know all about the complications, Dad. Luke had a sit-down with me and explained, and then there's Karen, who is always talking at me, trying to fix me, talking about you and me. I just don't understand why she gives you a pass after you walked out the way you did. I wouldn't be so understanding."

Right, his son wasn't about to make this easy for him at all.

"You can be angry at me, but don't question Karen's understanding," Raymond said. "She's my daughter, and you're my son. I love each of you deeply, and yes, this is damn complicated, every aspect of this family, but make no mistake—we're a family…"

"Until you're gone again," Brady snapped, cutting him off and standing.

Iris hesitated as she strode into the living room, and Brady gave everything to her with one look as if she were the parent instead of Raymond.

"I'm going out," he said.

Iris just pulled in a breath and nodded. "Fine, but be back for dinner. Everyone's coming over, and it looks like neither you nor Luke did much in the way of shopping."

Brady shrugged. "If you want me to go to the store, I'll go."

Iris shook her head. "No, it's fine. I'll figure out what we need. Just answer your phone and be back before dinner."

Then his son was gone, and Iris took one step and another and stopped just in front of him.

"Well, that went well," she said. "I could hear everything in the kitchen. Suzanne's on her way over, but I'm thinking of driving to Marcus and Charlotte's to just check in and see if there's something I can do."

The mother bear. That was just the way Iris was around her children.

"Since I can't do anything here, how about I tag along?" Raymond said.

Iris stepped closer, holding out her hand, and he reached for it and held it, taking in the smile he loved to see on her face. "If you want," she said.

He stood up and took in his son, who was pulling on his coat at the front door, a frown on his face, wearing sneakers. He wondered if, in the back of his mind, he'd thought Brady would be the easy one. Then Brady stepped out of the house and pulled the door closed, and he felt Iris's hand on his shoulder and pulled his gaze back to her.

"Give him time," she said, staring up at him, her expression serious. "He'll come around."

He glanced down at her. "I'm not so sure about that."

All Iris did was rub her hand over his arm and look over to the door, then back to him. "Well, I am, because I went through that very same angry stage with every one of the kids—in a different way, of course. Every time, I thought we'd never get past it. But we did, and so will you and Brady. Now let's go."

She pulled her hand away, and he found himself watching this woman he loved, his wife, whom he'd left to raise their kids alone. He didn't know why, but her saying that one thing eased some of the worry he hadn't realized he'd been holding on to about Brady, about all his kids.

CHAPTER

Ten

"We should call your family," Jack said.

Karen was lying on a gurney in a dark room, waiting for an ultrasound, as the doctor had agreed with Jack that they needed to confirm the fetus wasn't viable. She stared at the ceiling, feeling the quiet of the room as Jack's hand rested on her forehead. She closed her eyes to his touch.

"Why?" she said. "We'll have the ultrasound, confirm everything I know, and go home. You should call Marcus about Charlotte, see if she had the baby, talk to them. You shouldn't tell anyone about this, though. It would take away from Marcus and Charlotte's happy day. No one needs to know."

There was just something about knowing her brother and Charlotte were having a baby and she wasn't. She didn't want to think about it too long.

"If that's what you want," Jack said. "I still think your family needs to know, though."

She turned her head just as the door opened and the lab technician stepped inside.

"Okay, are you ready to get started?" she said.

"We are," Jack answered for her.

The tech pulled up her gown and squirted cold jelly on Karen's belly. She said something else to her, but Karen had stopped listening. It appeared Jack was talking for her, as it took her only a moment to realize the technician didn't know all the details.

"Just having a look here…" she said as she pressed the wand to Karen's abdomen. The monitor was turned away so Karen couldn't see. Then the tech pulled away the wand, slid it back into a slot by the monitor, and switched it off. "Okay, I think we're done," was all she said before wiping off the rest of the jelly with a towel. "You can get dressed, and your doctor will talk with you."

When she walked out of the room, Karen pulled in a breath and looked over to Jack, who wasn't smiling but had slid his hand over her arm.

"Come on, get up," he said. "Let's talk to the doctor."

Karen let Jack help her up, and she slid around on the bed in the hospital gown, tossing the paper blanket to the side. She stood up and pulled off the gown, then tossed it on the gurney, standing in her bra as Jack handed her the long-sleeved shirt she'd worn. She pulled it over her head, then pulled up the sweats and underwear that she had pulled low, below her pelvic bone. She sat in the chair as she reached for her sneakers and shoved her socked feet into them. Jack was holding her purse and her coat, and he slid his arm around her and guided her to the door, pressing a kiss to the side of her head.

"I know you want to wallow, but I know you, Karen. Maybe you should call your mom and talk to her…"

She reached for the door and pulled it open. Jack's hand went to the frame, holding it above her head. He was so much taller than her as they stepped into the hallway, and he was still holding her coat and purse. He reached for her hand then and linked their fingers, and she slowed her pace as she took in the sterile hall of the hospital.

"You think me talking to my mom's going to help?"

He pulled her to a stop just before the desk where they had checked in for the ultrasound, seeing the staff back there. She wanted to just go home.

"I think if you're not going to talk to me, you need to talk to someone," he said. "Why not your mom? I know how close you are, all of you. You don't want to tell anyone else right now to steal the limelight from Marcus and Charlotte, even though I think your family wouldn't agree…"

"Karen, Jack," Doctor Breckenridge called out. She had dark hair tied back, a strong, confident woman. She gestured them over to the side of the hall. "So, as I said, the baby isn't viable. It happens sometimes, one of those things. You have a couple of choices: You can go home and wait for it to pass on its own, or we can schedule you in now and take care of it here in the hospital."

The doctor glanced only a second to Jack before looking back at her. Right, it was her decision. Jack was still holding her hand, and maybe the reality of where she was and what had happened was why she was having some trouble trying to figure things out.

"And you want me to decide right now?" she said. Even she could hear the edge to her voice.

Doctor Breckenridge shook her head. "You can wait a few days, see if it passes on its own. Don't feel pressured here, Karen. It's entirely your choice."

"Well, that's the thing. I do feel pressured. I never asked you, but did I do something to cause this?"

The doctor pressed a hand to her shoulder, moving

them closer to the wall, the only privacy they could find. She felt awkward. Jack was so close, and he didn't walk away or pull his hand from hers.

"No, this happens more than you know, Karen," the doctor said. "It's just one of those things, so don't think you did something. We don't know why it happens. Often, it's nature's way of taking care of something that was wrong with the fetus. As I said to you, there's no reason you can't start trying again after this."

She said nothing, just felt Jack squeezing her hand.

"We're here now in the hospital, Karen," he said. "If you'd rather we do this now, come on."

At his urging, she wondered how he could be so calm.

He turned to the doctor. "Can you schedule it now?"

The doctor was still looking at her, then over to Jack. "Yeah, we'll get you checked in, Karen, and it shouldn't be more than a few hours. You can be home tonight."

All Karen did was nod, because she couldn't find the words.

"Just pop in down the hall at admissions, and they'll get you checked in and see you soon," the doctor said. Then she was walking away.

"Well, that was easy," Karen said.

Jack was now standing in front of her, his hand on her arm, holding everything together. "Nothing easy about it, but let's move on and get you checked in. You sure you don't want me to call anyone?" He handed her purse to her as they strode down the hall, his arm around her.

She heard her phone ding, so she reached in and saw she had a voicemail and a missed call. Jack said nothing as she pressed the phone to her ear and listened.

"Hey, darlin'." It was her dad. "Just wanted to let you know we're back. Call me when you get this. Your mom is talking to Suzanne right now. She misses all of you and wants to see everyone tonight."

She wasn't sure why hearing her dad's voice had her suddenly stopping in the hall. She pulled the phone away, looking down at the floor as she shoved it back in her purse.

"Who was it?" Jack asked, always reasonable.

"They're back," she said, then lowered her voice as she turned around. "My dad," she continued quietly, and she wasn't sure what to make of his expression.

He only nodded and then said, "Come on," as he reached for her hand and pulled her along toward admissions. They would check her in and take care of the problem so they could move on.

But she was having a hard time adopting that reasonable way of thinking.

***

KAREN WAS in a darkened private room in the hospital, in a gown, lying in bed. She blinked, feeling a hand touch hers, and she looked over, expecting Jack, but it was her dad standing there.

"Dad, how..." She was still feeling groggy from the local anesthetic and was resting. Just as the doctor said, the procedure had been done quickly, so clinical and final.

"Hey, there, darlin'. Jack called. I dropped your mom off at Marcus and Charlotte's. She's home, resting. Labor hasn't started. I just heard about what happened."

She wasn't sure why she was falling apart as she felt tears burn her eyes. She wasn't a crier. She felt her face crumple.

"Hey, it's okay." He was holding her hand and pressed his other over her head, running it over her hair.

She pulled in a breath, sniffing loudly. "I'm sorry. I don't know why I'm doing this. I shouldn't be acting this way. I was barely pregnant…"

"Karen, you have every right to feel this way. This was a shitty thing. I could say all the right things, if you want—that you'll be okay, because you will, and you'll try again. But it probably won't help to hear that this happens, because you really don't need to hear that right now. Just know that I'm here. We're here."

She swiped her hand roughly over her eyes and nose, then forced a laugh. "I guess the emotions are from hormones and such. I'm not a crier, but I seem to be doing more of that lately."

Her dad handed her a Kleenex, and she took in the beard, glasses, and ball cap he was wearing.

"So is this your new look?"

He forced a smile. "Yeah, something like that. We'll talk about that later."

"Where's Jack?" She glanced to the closed door.

Her dad let his gaze linger on her for another second as he stood there, looking down on her, then gestured to the door. "He stepped out when I got here. He called me and said you needed to talk to me. Would've thought you'd call your mom, but I'm glad he called me. You know your mom miscarried too—twice, actually, once after Marcus, then after Suzanne. She took it hard both times, but she got past it, and you will too."

She knew she was frowning. "Mom never said anything."

Her dad crossed his arms, and she heard the rustle of his coat as he pulled it off and tossed it on the chair beside the bed. "No, she just moved on. We moved on. We had you, six of you. Your mom never had to say anything, but I knew she always wondered. It was just something there, something she didn't talk about."

"So what am I supposed to do now, Dad, just brush it off and move on? Try again?"

Her dad reached for her hand. "If you and Jack want kids, then yeah. Karen, you are so much like your mother in some ways, but in others, you're not. Lying there in that bed, you're my little girl…" He sighed. "I'm so sorry this happened to you."

She sniffed as her dad took her hand again.

"You should talk to your mom," he said. "She'd want to know."

She just shook her head. "Not right now. Charlotte's baby…?"

Her dad sat at the edge of the bed. "Not yet. It seems the baby's not ready, but it will be soon. It's okay to be sad, Karen, for yourself and what you and Jack lost, and be okay at the same time for Marcus and Charlotte. Your mom wants to see you all tonight, but I can tell her you won't be coming."

The door opened, and Jack strode in, looking at her dad before letting his gaze linger on her. "I signed your paperwork. We can go home. You can rest."

She pressed the back of her hand to her forehead and pulled in a breath, seeing Jack and her dad standing there, looking down on her. She shook her head. "I don't think me going home to rest alone with my thoughts is what I want. Yeah, this sucks, but I want to see Mom and everyone."

Her dad was giving her everything, and he nodded, but Jack shook his head.

"You heard the doctor," Jack said. "She said to take a couple days and rest. I don't think it's a good idea."

"I disagree," was all she said back to him.

Her dad stepped in, leaned down, and pressed a kiss to her forehead. "Well, I'll leave you two to figure out the logistics, but it depends on where Charlotte is, as your mom wanted all of you over. We'll stock up. One more thing: Luke has his lady friend over. He brought her home for all of you to meet properly."

The way her dad said it, she knew there was something more.

"Well, before you talk to your brothers," he said, "you should know that Rosemary is the sister of Ben Schwartz."

She didn't know that name. She dragged her gaze over to Jack, and the way he shook his head had her saying, "I don't know who that is. Can one of you please tell me what the problem is?"

Jack slid his gaze back to her and stepped closer. "He was the man who broke into your brother's place and held a gun at Iris and Eva, who would've killed them."

For a second, she thought he was kidding.

When she glanced to her dad at the door, he just shrugged. "We've all done something, Karen, but remember that Rosemary wasn't involved in that," he said, then stepped out, and she just stared at Jack, trying to wrap her head around why and how.

"Do you think Marcus knows?" she said. When she sat up in the bed, she felt the discomfort and winced. Jack was there, his hand on her.

"I don't know, but are you sure you still want to go?"

The way he said it, it took her another second to realize he was serious. "Of course I do. That's my family. I don't know what was going through Luke's head, but I guess Dad's right; she didn't do it. But still, I know Marcus, and I'm not sure he'll see it that way."

Jack merely grunted and glanced over to the closed door, then back to her. "Okay, come on. Let's get you dressed and home, and then, I guess, if you still feel like it, we'll show up at your mom's and stay for whatever fallout I expect will happen."

CHAPTER

Eleven

"Grandma, what's it like being on the run?" Alison said.

Iris wiped down the island in Charlotte and Marcus's kitchen after cleaning up the dishes left from Marcus's breakfast and the snacking Alison had been doing. It wasn't a big mess, but cleaning was one thing she could do to help.

Raymond had dropped her off after Jack called him. Why, she still didn't know, but she had told him to go, because being here with Charlotte was the only place she wanted to be right now.

"You make me sound like a criminal," she said. "I assure you it's not that glamourous."

Alison shrugged and didn't pull those dark eyes from her. Iris didn't know why, but she wondered whose eyes the baby would have. She glanced up to the ceiling, taking in how quiet it was.

"Well, it's not how I pictured my life would be," she continued, "but the problem is that when you plan every-thing and think it's going to fit into a mold and be simple and easy, that's when life smacks you upside the head and goes in an entirely different direction. But you know that already, don't you?"

"You're not really answering me," Alison said. "You're sounding a little too philosophical, like Dad does when he doesn't want to give me a straight answer." She was so damn smart, too smart for her own good.

"Okay, fair enough. I never expected to have a second chance with Raymond, but I do, and I'm taking it how I get it. You know enough, Alison, about how things work, and you've seen the bad people who exist in this world, who have made it impossible for him to be who he is. So we can't slip…"

"You mean he's your new boyfriend? Yeah, I got it, Jake from California. It's twisted, Grandma."

Even though it sounded as if she wasn't on board, Iris knew her granddaughter thought it was absolutely cool, this cloak and dagger kind of stuff.

"Maybe so," she said, "but I'm happy. The only problem is, as you put it, being on the run and having to move around so as not to be noticed. It isn't what I expected, but as long as I can come back and see you all often, I'm fine with it. So yes, he's my boyfriend, and I'm only a phone call away. You know that. I told you before. So tell me about you and the fact that I know you're skipping school right this minute?"

Alison shrugged again. "Marcus needed someone to stay with Charlotte, and I told my mom I didn't want to go today. I'm caught up, and it's just a bunch of stuck-up kids there, anyway."

Okay, so her teenage misfit granddaughter was still not fitting in.

"So how about Brady? How are things going with him?" she said, but then she thought she heard Charlotte upstairs by the creak of the floor. "Hold that thought—but I can tell by your expression that you two haven't figured things out."

"There's nothing to talk about, Grandma. It's awkward. He's, like, my dad's brother. I'm having to answer questions at school about why Brady and I are on the outs and avoiding each other, and hearing that I must've done something hurts more than anything, because I can't even explain the truth, which is that this sick, twisted universe is all about flipping me the middle finger and saying, 'Screw you, Alison. We'll make sure you're never happy.' He's the one guy I really like, and suddenly I'm related to him. Like, that's a one in ten million thing. It never happens. But it happened to us."

Iris was stunned as she took in her granddaughter, realizing she was stuck in a dark place. She glanced up to the ceiling, hearing the footsteps, and stared for another second at Alison. "Oh, boy, put the kettle on," she said. "Seems I've missed a lot. You listen to me, though. We're talking about this, but you don't hold a monopoly on getting screwed around. You're not the only one this happens to. The Brady thing… Yeah, I don't know what to say to that, because if I were you, I'd likely be thinking the same thing. Except, from where I'm standing, I can see a very different story and outcome for you. Let me check on Charlotte. You make the tea and rummage through the cupboards, see if there's anything good to go with it."

Alison said nothing else.

Iris had reached the stairs and was looking up when she spotted Charlotte, barefoot in sweats, coming down.

"Iris, I thought I heard you," she said. "I can't believe you're here." She walked slowly, awkwardly, holding the rail and making a face. She couldn't hide her discomfort.

"Wasn't going to miss the arrival of my grandchild," Iris said. "How are you feeling? Did you get any sleep?"

Charlotte shook her head as she stepped off the last stair. "Some, but not much. Just rested a bit. My back has been aching something fierce. No matter how much I move and which side I lie on, I can't get comfortable."

Iris had her hand on Charlotte's back just as Alison appeared, holding a teapot and box of tea.

"Oh, hi, Charlotte. I'm making tea. Do you want some?"

"You know, I'll take a glass of water instead. Thanks, Alison. Where is Marcus?"

They walked into the living room, Iris following her, and she could hear the kettle now whistling as Alison went back into the kitchen.

"Alison said he was called in to handle something. Do you want me to call him?" Iris asked.

Charlotte sat in the old wood rocking chair that had been hers, which one of her kids had refinished. "No, it's fine. He's just going to worry because we're playing the waiting game…" She stopped talking, and Iris took in her discomfort, knowing when a woman was in labor.

Just then, the front door opened to reveal Raymond, with snow on his hair and jacket, which he brushed off as he strode in and closed the door behind him.

"It's really coming down out there," he said. "Everyone okay here?"

Iris sat on the sofa table in front of Charlotte, seeing how she clutched the arm of the chair. "We're good. Charlotte just woke up and came downstairs." She felt his hand touch her shoulder before she could say anything else.

"She's in labor?" he said.

She glanced up. "Yeah, appears so."

Charlotte blew out a breath, rested her hand on her

very pregnant belly, and said, as if it had taken her by surprise, "I think maybe you should call Marcus now."

"That's a good idea," Raymond said as he pulled out his phone.

Iris reached for Charlotte's hand and squeezed. "Is this the first one you've had?" She lifted her watch and took in the time.

"Yeah, just my back upstairs, nothing like this."

Raymond was standing right there. "Marcus, if you get this message, we're at your house, and Charlotte's in labor. It's time you came home."

"It went to voicemail?" Charlotte said, then made a face at another contraction.

Iris just looked up to Raymond, who jutted his chin to the window. All she could see was white outside.

"I'm not sure we should wait," Raymond said. "If I remember with you, by the time we had Suzanne, we barely made it to the hospital, and the roads out there aren't good. I think we should pack her up, and I'll call Marcus and tell him to meet us there."

Iris stood up, seeing how serious Raymond was. It took only one look out the window and another back to Charlotte to know he was absolutely right.

CHAPTER

Twelve

"I never figured you for someone who would run away, Rosemary," Luke said.

Her hair was still damp, and she was shoving her makeup kit in her suitcase. Her clothes were rolled and neatly packed, and she flipped the suitcase closed and zipped it up. She wore a white V-neck sweater and blue jeans.

She said nothing as she went to lift her suitcase off his neatly made bed, with its blue and brown quilt. A small desk in the corner and a tall chest of drawers were the only other furniture, and the only thing he'd stuck up on the wall were photos of his team and some places he'd been, including his favorite, an off-the-road village in Yemen that most people would never have heard of.

"I'm not running away," she said. "I'm saving my dignity. I told you this could never work, and your brothers' responses last night were what I expected. No, actually, what I expected was worse, but still, I had to live my worst nightmares about your family's reaction to me. And you know what? I can't blame them. Seeing that little girl,

Eva… How could Ben have terrorized her like that? And your mom, I could see she was putting up a good front, but she was completely thrown. I know how to read people too, and your mom isn't comfortable with me. So I should go home. I should never have left. I don't want to face another attack from your family, your sisters, your brothers, who do not want me here. Even though I understand how your family feels, the fact is that I would never do what my brother did—and, just so you know, he wasn't always like that."

He could see she'd heard nothing he'd said, but he wondered, in the back of his mind, whether maybe she was right. "I understand how upset you are. I am too, because I didn't expect that response from my brothers, not like that. At the same time, I told you before that they didn't need to know anything about you being related to Ben, just like they have no idea of what really happened to make your brother, all of you, come for retribution."

"It wasn't retribution, Luke. We wanted to get my dad back. He was trying to do the right thing, but for this country, the right thing is not so black and white. Being a good guy and exposing corporate crime and greed like my dad tried to do will get you locked away in some hole, where you'll never be heard from again. I get how they can't know about that part, but how fair do you think that is?" she snapped, her voice low.

He was glad no one was home now. As she went to lift the suitcase from the bed, he reached for her hand, stopping her, actually pushing the suitcase away as he stepped closer to her. "It's not fair," he said. "You're right, and it sucks that they can't know everything that happened, but at the same time, there was no justification for what Ben did."

She crossed her arms, and the look on her face told him he was treading a fine line here.

"You know what I mean," he said.

"I know Ben felt that was the only way to get our dad back, and he was right." She flicked the flat of her hand in the air when he went to interrupt. "But we're debating what went down again. It's over. My dad is free, my brother is dead, and your mom and Eva are fine, but your family hates me. Now, if you don't mind, I'm leaving." She went to step around him, but he took another step toward her.

"And then what, we're over?" he said. He was touching her, holding her back, and he could feel her tension, her body. He loved being with her, everything about her. She was so damn complicated. This was why he'd asked her to come, because his dad had told him the one thing he'd never expected, to stop hiding her.

She wouldn't look at him. His cell phone rang, and he reached in his pocket and pulled it out, taking in the unknown number but having an idea who it was.

"Hey, what's going on?" he said.

"Charlotte's in labor," Raymond said. "Your mom and I are taking her to the hospital now. Left a message for Marcus, but he didn't answer. I know he was called in. We've got Alison, too. I want you to go and find your brother. Keep calling him, and tell him to meet us at the hospital. The way the snow is coming down, I'm not waiting to see if he got my message."

He looked over Rosemary's head, to the open door of his bedroom. "That's great," Luke said. "Sure, I'll track down Marcus and have him make his way to the hospital. Wow, so the baby's making an appearance."

"Yup," Raymond said. "Suzanne is calling Owen and Ryan and letting everyone know, but you find Marcus, call him, and if he won't answer, go and find him and get him to the hospital." Then his dad hung up.

Rosemary was still standing there, ready to go.

"That was my dad," Luke said. "Charlotte's in labor this time. They're taking her to the hospital. It's snowing pretty heavy out, so they're not waiting. Look, I get what you're saying, and I understand, but I know my family. Since you wanted them to know and dropped the knowledge on them like a bomb, you didn't give them a chance to get their heads around it…"

She said nothing, just stood there, her arms crossed, and he wasn't sure what she was thinking.

"I have to track down Marcus," he continued. "Let's just table this for now, this discussion and the idea of you leaving, because in case you haven't looked outside, the snow is really coming down. There's no way you should be driving out there right now. Let me find my brother, and I promise you, if my family doesn't come around, you and I will leave, and I'll drive you back to Indiana the same way I drove you up here."

"I can drive myself back to Indiana," she said, "but go and call your brother."

He didn't know if that meant she'd wait or that she was still leaving.

"Go call him," she said again, and he stepped out of the bedroom and into the hallway, hearing the front door open as he started dialing Marcus's number. Brady entered, covered in snow and shaking off his coat.

"Hey, Charlotte's in labor," Luke told him. "Heard you and your dad had a talk. How'd it go?"

Brady said nothing, and a gloomy expression lurked on his face.

"That good, huh?" Luke said. Great, just one more person in this house who wasn't making anything easy. He listened as Marcus's phone went right to voicemail. "Hey, it's Luke," he said. "Charlotte's in labor, and I've been tasked with tracking you down and getting you to the hospital. Just where the hell are you? Call me back."

He hung up the phone, and immediately after, his phone rang and he saw Marcus's caller ID.

"Where are you?" was all he got out.

"Charlotte's in labor?" Marcus said.

"Yeah, I got a call from Dad. He and mom are taking Charlotte to the hospital now, with the snow on the roads. You know the story. Don't think they want to take a chance on waiting for you. Where are you?"

"I'm at that park outside downtown, where the homeless camp is, clearing it out. Look, I'm on my way. Heads up, Ryan filled me in on your little stunt. You seriously brought the sister of the man who would've killed Eva and Mom without blinking an eye into my house? I always knew you weren't quite right in the head, Luke, but this is too much. Tell me you've got your head on straight now and have sent her on her way."

He turned his back, walking into the living room, seeing the open curtains and the near whiteout conditions. Okay, it was worse than he thought on both fronts. "Hey, ease up. She's not her brother, and it wasn't her with the gun. I don't appreciate you calling me out, thinking I'd bring someone dangerous around, and you never asked what it was my team did to bring this down on all of you."

Marcus swore on the other end.

"Look, you need to get your ass to the hospital," Luke continued. "Mom and Dad have Charlotte, so how about we table the other argument until after the baby? You should know Rosemary wants to leave…"

"Good. She should," Marcus snapped, cutting him off,

and that was the first time Luke would've put a fist in his brother's face if he'd been standing there in front of him.

"I'm going to let that go only because you're stressed that you're about to be a father and aren't thinking clearly. Before you say something else you can't take back, I'm going to hang up," he said, and then he did.

When he turned, both Brady and Rosemary were standing in the living room, likely having heard at least one side of that conversation.

"Well, who's up for ordering pizza?" he said.

"In a snowstorm?" Rosemary added.

Brady shrugged. "I could eat a pizza."

"Great, put your coats on."

Rosemary looked at him as if he were crazy. "Why?"

"As you said, there's a snowstorm, so I'm not letting some newly licensed pizza delivery kid driving some run-down piece of shit on bald tires drive a pizza out to us. We'll go pick one up, and we'll stop for some beer, too."

And then what? Maybe he'd have some time to figure out just how he was supposed to solve the situation with Rosemary and his family.

"You want to grab something to eat on the way home?" Jack said. "I'll pick something up, and you can put your feet up for a bit. Maybe you'll reconsider going out. You sure you want to go to your mom's tonight?"

Jack never fussed over her as he was now. She felt his hand lingering on her back as they walked down the hospital hall. Her coat was on, and she was done, checked out. There was just something about all of this being over. It filled her with no peace. She was unsettled, rattled, just reminding herself to put one foot in front of the other as they rounded the corner to the entrance.

"I could eat," she said. "I'm hungry, but I don't want to stop anyplace. I want to go home and have a shower, but I also want to see my family. I don't want to stay home and stare at a wall. In case I didn't say it, thanks for calling my dad." She stopped and turned in the circle of his arms, looking up into his icy blue eyes, which had softened. She could see the worry there. "But we should also talk about this governor thing. You said we have to move. Are you sure there's no way out of it?"

His arm was around her again, and he started walking with her. The hallway was busy with staff and patients, and she slid her arm around Jack's waist, leaning against him as they walked slowly, no hurry.

"A deal is just that," he said. "I knew what I was agreeing to, Karen. Just didn't think it would happen this fast. I gave my word—but think of it this way. I'm not a puppet. They want to put me there, and that's what I agreed to, but that doesn't mean I'm going to be a figurehead who allows every dirty agenda of theirs to be pushed through. I'll agree to something only if it's something I can sleep with at night."

A politician. It was such a dirty word, yet her husband was on his way to being one. She'd never expected for this to be a part of her life.

"So how soon are we talking?" she said. "Because we're still working on cases. I have Henderson's custody, and then there's Tyler Evan's trial coming up on those fraud charges, and…"

"Hey, I know we have a full case load, but we have to start scaling down. We'll finish the cases we have, but we'll have to refer some that we can't. I have to be in Missoula at week's end, when the meetings start. For now, I'll be commuting until we can close up shop. There are other things to talk about, like where you'll practice. I know you didn't want to work at my law firm in Missoula, where I'm still a partner, but…"

She was looking up at him, shaking her head.

"Okay, never mind," he said. "But you know I can make a spot there for you."

"And you know I'm not a corporate lawyer, Jack. I never want to be in a firm where the people I want to help can't afford me. You think I want to work for the kinds of people who can afford the hourly rate your firms boasts? That's not why I became a lawyer, Jack. I think my mother raised me better. I just wanted more time."

He said nothing else as they approached the door at the end. When it slid open, she could see the snow coming down outside—and there was Marcus. Her stomach zinged as he spotted them and started their way.

"Did you tell Marcus we were here?" she said.

"Nope…" was all Jack replied.

Her brother brushed the snow off his hair, looking right and left as he approached. "Did Mom and Dad call you?" he said.

Karen just blinked, taking in her brother, who appeared off, frazzled.

"Look, Charlotte's in labor," he said. "Have you seen them? Were you up there?"

The last thing she wanted to talk about was why she was there. "Oh, that's great! No, I haven't seen them. So Charlotte's here?"

Marcus ran his hand over his hair again, taking in Jack and then Karen and narrowing his gaze. "Yeah, Luke called me, said they were trying to get a hold of me and they didn't want to wait with the snow on the road. They must be up there. So you haven't seen them? How come you're here, then?"

Karen looked up to Jack, knowing he was aware she didn't want Marcus knowing why she was there.

"No, did you check with admissions?" Jack said, jutting his chin to the admissions desk just ahead of them.

Marcus said nothing else as he walked over, and she followed with Jack, appreciating that he hadn't answer Marcus's question. They stood just behind him, listening to him question the admissions lady.

"Your sure Charlotte O'Connell isn't here?" he said. "She's in labor. My family brought her in and are meeting me here. They should be here. Please check again."

At the urgency in his voice, Karen felt so out of the loop. She pulled her phone out of her purse and powered it on.

"Who're you calling?" Jack asked in a low voice.

Marcus was leaning on the counter, and the clerk was checking the computer again. She could see her brother gesturing to her to turn the computer screen so he could see it. Maybe now wasn't the time to point out the illegality of that.

"I'm calling Mom to see where they are," she said. She had her phone to her ear, and it rang but only went to voicemail. "Hey, Mom, it's Karen. We're at the hospital, and Marcus is here, but Charlotte isn't. He said you're bringing her, so I'm just checking to see where you are." Then she hung up.

Marcus was tapping the counter, and he had his phone out, as well.

"She's not here?" Karen asked. "I just called Mom, and it went to voicemail."

Marcus was dialing his phone. "I don't like this…" he said. "Hey, where are you? I'm at the hospital. Call me back, as I'm getting a little worried." He shook his head, and she could see his frustration.

"Who'd you call?" she asked.

He just gestured to her and then Jack. "The old man," he said. "No answer. You said Mom didn't answer, either… I'll try Charlotte, but I don't like it that they can't pick up their damn phones, especially when they have my very pregnant wife in labor with them!" Then he had his phone to his ear again.

She looked up to Jack. "I'll call Luke and let him know," she said. "Why don't you call Harold?"

It seemed they all had their phones out, and she took in Marcus shaking his head as she listened to Luke's phone ring.

"What's going on?" he answered.

"Hey, we're at the hospital with Marcus. He said you called him about Charlotte in labor and she was on her way to the hospital, but she's not here. I tried calling Mom, but it went to voicemail." She was pretty sure, by the way Marcus shook his head, that his annoyance was quickly giving way to the kind of frustration she hadn't seen on her brother's face in a long time. "You have any idea where they are?"

"No, I have no idea. I got a call they were heading to the hospital, but they should be there by now. I was tasked with tracking down Marcus and getting him there, so my duty's done. They could be there any minute, but the roads are bad. I'm out with the kid and Rosemary. We're just waiting on a pizza we ordered. Got to tell you, we were almost sideswiped by a car that slid right through an inter-section. Why don't I backtrack and see if I can find them, and you'll call me if they show up?"

She only nodded, unsure of who Marcus was calling now, who he was talking to. "Yeah, do that. I'll call you as soon as they walk in. Hopefully, you're right." Then she hung up.

Jack was shaking his head. "Owen is there with Harold. He said both are going to make their way here, and Ryan too. They'll keep an eye out for them…"

"That was Suzanne," Marcus said. "She's going to call around, call a few of the buddies she still talks to at the fire department. We're probably overreacting…"

She reached over and touched Marcus's arm. "You're

entitled to worry. I'm sure they'll walk in here any minute. You likely just beat them here. You probably flashed your lights, ran the siren to move people out of the way, and drove faster than you should, right?"

There it was, just the hint of a smile.

"Ah, see? I know you well."

"Fine, I'll give you that, but at the same time, why aren't they answering? Charlotte, I can see, but Mom makes no sense, and Dad? With the snowstorm outside and the fact that my wife is in labor and I don't know where the hell she is…" He blew out a breath.

The words that always came easy for her had deserted her now. "Luke is looking, and Ryan, Owen, and Harold are on their way. Just take a breath and try to relax, because there's nothing you can do, so how about not panicking? We'll give them a little longer before we start talking about sounding the alarm."

He just took her in, then Jack, and pulled in a breath. "Fine, I guess you're right—but wait a second. You're both here, so who called you two, and how did you get here before me?"

It was the one thing she didn't want to answer. Marcus dragged his gaze from her to Jack and then back, and Karen, for the life of her, couldn't figure out what to say.

"Okay, what's going on?" Marcus said. "I can see something is up. I've got time, here. As you see, I'm waiting. Someone did call you, right?"

Karen couldn't get her tongue to move. She glanced up to Jack, who gave everything to her before looking back over to Marcus.

"We'll talk about that another time," Jack said. "Right now, this is about your wife…"

"You're scaring me," Marcus said. "What's going on?

My wife isn't here, so how about you tell me? Karen, Jack, come on, what is it?"

This wasn't how she wanted anyone to find out.

She breathed out. "I was pregnant and miscarried," she said, then nothing else. She pulled her bottom lip between her teeth and bit down. She didn't have to wonder what Marcus was thinking, as his expression said everything. "And you know what? If it's all the same, Marcus, I don't want to talk about it, and I don't want anyone else to know."

Iris wasn't sure what she was looking at. She felt something pressing into her face, and it took another second for her to realize she was in the car, and it was the airbag. She couldn't breathe as she pressed at the bulky fabric, trying to get it away from her and give her the space she needed to wiggle out.

She leaned back, looking to the side window, seeing nothing but snow. She could hear the sounds of the car, the whirring of the engine, and Charlotte cried out behind her.

"Grandma, Grandma, wake up!"

She heard the panic in Alison's voice and felt the pull of the seatbelt, but for a moment, she couldn't figure out how to move. She felt her seat back being shaken.

"Grandma, wake up! Charlotte, please say something!"

"I'm okay," Iris said. "I just can't move this damn airbag…" She fisted her hand, pushing the airbag down and away, then turned to see Raymond slumped behind the wheel beside her. "Are you okay, Alison, Charlotte?" she cried out. "Talk to me. What the hell happened?"

Why couldn't she remember? They had been driving, and she was looking over the seatback to Charlotte, who'd been in labor. Her contractions were strong. She'd been timing them, she thought. The next thing she knew, here they were. What the hell had happened?

She looked around, trying to figure out where they were, and she reached over and touched Raymond. "Raymond, wake up, are you okay?" she said. She pressed her hand over the airbag. She'd never known that this was how they deployed. It took her another second to realize they were in a ditch, she thought, by the way she was leaning against the door. It was an odd angle.

"Alison, are you okay?" she called out, reaching down and unlatching her seatbelt.

Beside her, Raymond was stirring. There was a cut on his forehead, and blood, and the glasses he was wearing were broken. He pulled them off.

"Raymond, are you okay, and Charlotte?" She somehow turned in her seat and could see Charlotte still belted in the back behind Raymond, leaning back and groaning in agony. With the angle of the car, she and Alison were higher than she was. "Oh, no, no, no, Charlotte, are you hurt?"

"Grandma, when that semi lost control, it was coming right at us. I thought it hit us. We spun around and hit the ditch," Alison said.

Iris somehow managed to move back her seat. There was no way her door was opening. By the angle they were in the ditch, her door was pressed against a snowbank or something. She slipped around on her knees so she could see the panicked look on her granddaughter's face, then glanced over to Charlotte, who was shaking her head, her teeth clenched. Iris's head banged the roof of the car, and there just wasn't enough room as she leaned over the armrest between the front seats.

"Oh, the contractions are so strong now," Charlotte said. "I can't wait. I feel the baby. It's coming…"

"Alison, can you climb over Charlotte and get out her door?" Iris said. She reached over and touched Raymond's shoulder as he shook his head. She could tell that he had hit it, as he was blinking again, maybe confused. "Raymond, come on, talk to me."

"What the hell…?" was all he said as he lifted his hand and touched his head.

Alison, in just her hoodie, was trying to climb over Charlotte in the back seat, where there wasn't a lot of room. Iris heard her yanking on the door, and she thought she heard her cell phone ringing, but it was in her purse on the floor. She couldn't reach it.

"Is everyone okay?" Raymond called out.

"It won't open, Grandma!" Alison said.

"Oh no…" Charlotte cried out and groaned.

Iris knew her labor was active and hard, and this wasn't the spot to be having her baby. She couldn't reach her. She felt Raymond's hand on her and heard him yanking on the door, pushing against it again and again. When it opened, all she could see was snow and a jackknifed semi on the road above. Raymond pushed on the airbag and somehow slid out, and she thought he fell in the snow, which had to be deep.

"Alison, where's your phone?" Iris said. "Do you have it on you?"

"Yeah, right here."

"I want you to call for help right now. Call 911. And, Charlotte, we're going to get you out of here." She leaned over the seat, seeing the seatbelt that was holding her there. She was about to push it, but with the angle she was being held, she didn't think that was wise. She pressed her hand to Charlotte's leg, hearing sirens in the distance.

"Grandma, they said an ambulance has already been called and is coming…"

"Give me the phone." She reached for it, her hand resting on Charlotte's leg. She could feel the car being rocked, knowing Raymond was trying to yank open the back door, Charlotte's door. She felt the car move, and her stomach bottomed out in horror. Alison screamed.

"Raymond, stop!" Iris yelled, and he must have heard, as he stopped pulling and leaned his head in as she pressed the phone to her ear.

"Ma'am, hello, are you there?" It was the dispatcher.

"Yes, this is Iris O'Connell. My granddaughter just told you we were in an accident. We went off the road. We were on the way to the hospital. It's on…" She slipped the phone from her mouth and shouted, "Raymond, where are we, exactly?"

"Highway 3, just off the main road," he said, leaning in and touching the seat.

She looked back at Charlotte as she said, "Did you hear that? We're on Highway 3, just off the main road. I have the wife of Sheriff Marcus O'Connell in the back. She's in active labor. I need you to send EMTs. The back door won't open, and her contractions are right on top of another, too close. My…" She stopped before she said "husband," feeling the panic at the fact that he'd slipped already. He was Jake to the public, not Raymond. This was exactly what he'd hammered into her. "We can't get the back door open. We tried, but the car was slipping. I'm not sure if it's a ditch or a hill…"

"Listen, you stay where you are and don't move," the dispatcher said. "We've got help on the way. Someone already called about you. We'll notify the sheriff, as well. I need you to stay on the phone with me until they get there."

"Okay, I'm putting my granddaughter back on," she said, and gestured to Alison, who was wide-eyed, kneeling on the seat, her hand on her seatback.

"Iris, I can't hold it. I feel the baby…" Charlotte yelled and groaned over and over. Iris knew the wailing and keening. They had to get her moved. She couldn't even deliver where she was.

"Okay, Charlotte, I need you to calm down," she said. "Help is on the way right now, so don't panic. We're going to have you out in no time and then to the hospital, and you'll have the baby. Everything's going to be fine."

"I don't want to have the baby here," she said. "It's too cold."

This was the worst-case scenario. She could see the lights, hear the sirens, and then Raymond was poking his head in the door.

"We broke through the guardrail, Iris," he said. "I need everyone not to move at all. One slip of the car, and it's over the edge. Alison, you hear me, Charlotte?" He leaned in over the seat. "I'm sorry. We'll get you out. Just try not to move…"

By the way he paused and looked at her, Iris knew it was worse than he was saying.

"I'll be right back," was all he said.

She just nodded, careful as she leaned back. She could see the firetruck and lights through the open door, but she heard the crunch of the snow, an awful sound, and felt the car moving beneath her. She felt something below her that left her with a sinking feeling as the car slipped again, then stopped. She heard yelling outside as she stayed where she was, leaning over the seat back, her hand on Charlotte's leg.

"Grandma, the car moved…!" Alison cried out, still clutching the phone. Her fear was exactly what Charlotte didn't need to hear.

"Don't move," Iris said. "We're going to be fine. Alison, I need you to tell the 911 operator that emergency services are here, and then I want you to hang up and don't move so we don't rock the car. We'll be fine. Help is here."

Charlotte was breathing heavy, looking to Alison and then over to her, fighting her own panic, likely with a very clear understanding of the situation they were in.

Metal creaking was a sound she wasn't familiar with, but it was something she'd never forget in this lifetime, ever —the grinding, the groan. Behind her, she could hear voices yelling, calling out, but all she could do was see the fear in both her granddaughter and Charlotte, hearing her breathing as the car moved again, jerking.

Terror filled the vehicle as she somehow reached for Charlotte's hand, because there was nothing she could do other than hold on to them and silently will that someone out there could do something to at least get Charlotte and Alison out.

Fifteen

Lights were flashing, snow was falling, and Luke saw a jackknifed semi and a car off the road, through the snapped guardrail. He knew well that on that part of the road, there were trees and then a sharp drop of at least thirty feet. He should have turned around, but there was just something about the car: He could make out the back of the light brown that blended in with the snow.

"You don't think it's them, do you?" was all Rosemary said.

They climbed out of the Jeep and saw the approaching emergency vehicles at the scene of the accident. Visibility was dipping close to zero, and a sheriff's car was approaching, wheels spinning and slipping. Luke turned to see Colby climbing out in a winter hat and jacket.

"Hey, you can't come through here," Colby shouted. "Get back in your vehicle and turn around."

Luke knew he didn't recognize him. "Colby, it's Luke. We're looking for Charlotte. She was with my mom, going to the hospital…" He didn't finish, though, because he spotted his dad by the car with the firefighters, arguing. He gestured to Colby. "Call Marcus! Charlotte's in that car, and she's in labor."

He didn't hear what the young deputy said as he strode past him, considering there wasn't a chance he was stopping him. He took in the rescue crew on the road and beyond the guard rail, seeing the odd angle the car had gone off the road. A line from one of the big trucks was hooked up to the bumper, but he knew that wouldn't hold the car if it went over. Another one was hooked to the guard rail as if to hold it in place.

"Dad…" Brady called out as they spotted Raymond standing there, his head cut. The EMTs were trying to keep them back. The driver's door was open, and one of the emergency team was leaning in. Luke couldn't make out who was inside. He couldn't see his mom, and the back door was closed.

Brady jogged past him, right to their dad, and he could see it was bad by the expression on Raymond's face.

"What happened here?" Luke called out. "Is everyone all right?"

Raymond had his arm around Brady and hugged him, then stepped away. When one of the EMTs stepped over and tried to press a bandage to his head, he said, "No, I'm fine. Help my family first." He lifted his hand to push back the young man, who was trying to do triage, but his dad was having none of it. "Charlotte's in labor and can't get the back door open. We went through a guardrail. We need to get in there and get them out. The car isn't stable —it's been slipping. Charlotte's contractions are close together. They need to get her out of there now…"

Yeah, his dad was worried. He could hear it in his voice, and he knew how dire this was.

"What happened here, Dad?" he said. He just took in the scene, the semi, the mangled tail of the car, which was steaming, and he felt a sick feeling. They needed another line around front to hold the car in place. They were working on getting the back door open. Precarious, indeed.

"The semi on the other side lost control, coming right for us. I tried to get around it, but the roads are slick and icy. He clipped the back end, and I spun. Tried to right it, but we went off the road…"

He didn't know what made him look, but he turned to see Marcus running their way. He glanced only once to Rosemary in her red knit hat and black wool coat, standing at the edge of the road, just watching the scene unfold.

"Hey, hey, Marcus, just hold up…" Luke was maybe two steps in front of Marcus, his hand on his shoulder.

"Get out of my way, Luke!" Marcus said, the warning clear, so Luke lifted his hands but moved with him.

"They're working on it, Marcus. The number-one priority is getting Charlotte out…"

But his brother wasn't listening.

"The door's stuck!" one of the fire crew yelled. "The car is slipping from the weight."

Luke turned to see Raymond behind him, the cut on his forehead bleeding, as well as Brady, as they waded into the ditch beyond the guard rail. Then Marcus was there at the car, even though one of the firefighters tried to hold him back. One of them had broken the back window, and he could see Charlotte after a blanket was pulled away. He could hear her loud and clear, a woman in labor, and he thought he heard Alison, too.

Keep it together, kid, he silently willed his niece.

"Hey, I'm going to get you out of here. You just hang in there, Charlotte," Marcus said, leaning in the window.

All Luke heard was the creak of metal as the emergency crew tried to secure the car. Marcus was holding the frame as if he could hold the entire car back. Luke took one step and another just as the emergency crews jammed a pole in through the window to try to pry the door open, but it was rocking the car.

"They're trying to get your mom out," his dad said as they watched the scene. One wrong move and the car would slip.

"Hey, easy there, guys!" he called out to the firefighters. "You're going to send the car over."

Just then, he heard the metal and the sound of the door opening.

"Luke, what's going on?"

He glanced back to see Harold and Ryan running their way, and Owen was back by where the EMT vehicle was parked, where Colby was likely trying to hold him back.

"Semi jackknifed and hit them. They went off the road. They're trying to get Charlotte out now…"

His mom was being helped out by one of the firefighters in front, but he could see she wasn't happy. "Why are you taking me out first?" she cried out. "I told you to get Charlotte!"

Luke reached for his mom's arm. "Mom, are you hurt?"

"No, but Charlotte isn't doing good," she said. "Luke, the baby is coming. They have to get her out of there. I don't know how long she can hold on…"

An EMT was right there. "We have to take you to the hospital and get you checked out," he said, but Luke could see his mom was ready to argue.

He gestured to Rosemary. "Come and stay with my mom," he called out. "Mom, you have to go and get checked out. We'll get Charlotte out. Don't worry."

He didn't know how, but they helped his mom up from the ditch, though she wouldn't go any further, standing there, watching the scene. He glanced only once to see that Rosemary was right there with her.

The back door was now open, and he couldn't get any closer without getting in the way. Marcus was there with the emergency crew, and he could see a backboard, could hear Charlotte as they pulled her out and strapped her onto it.

The car slipped again with a groan of metal, a sound he knew well. On pure instinct, with everyone yelling, he stepped in, his hand on the car. He knew Charlotte was being lifted out, and it was only for an instant, one second, that Alison's panicked eyes connected with his. The car shifted again with a loud crack that had him reaching in.

"Grab my hand!" he yelled. He was leaning in the front seat, reaching for the kid, her sweatshirt, her hand, her arm.

He yanked her, but the car was slipping. Everything went into slow motion. There was no time to think. This was what he did in messy situations. All he knew was that there was no way in hell he was letting her go. He pulled and felt his legs knocked out from under him as the car slid —and then he had her.

They fell back into the snow just as the car tipped. One second, then another, and it went over the edge.

"Stop shining that light in my eyes," Raymond snapped. "I told you I'm fine. You patched my head up, and I let you stitch me up. Now I want to go and check on my family."

He was behind a curtain in the emergency room, sitting on a gurney, and a young dark-haired doctor who hadn't shaved in a few days flicked off the penlight he'd been shining in his eyes.

"I'd prefer if you stayed overnight," the doctor said. "It seems you have a mild concussion…"

But Raymond was already shaking his head, not about to explain to this kid that he'd had way worse, and this was nothing. "Nope, I humored you, but I'm going." He slid off the gurney and looked down on the young doctor, who was a few inches shorter than him. "You know anything about Charlotte O'Connell?"

The man shook his head. "Not sure. I can check for you, if you like…"

"No, I'll find out," Raymond said.

"Go ask the nurses at the emergency station out front,"

the doctor said. "But no driving for at least a day or two, and rest, and if there's any change, a headache or anything, you come back."

He only nodded. He had no intention of following orders, because he was fine. It was everyone else he was worried about—his wife, Charlotte and the baby, and Alison.

He stepped out into the hall, and the first person he saw was Owen, with Iris sitting in a chair beside him.

"You okay?" he said to her.

Owen's gaze lingered, but he didn't say anything.

"I'm fine," Iris said. "We're just waiting to hear about Charlotte. They delivered the baby in the ambulance, Ryan said. It's a boy…"

He leaned down and reached for her hand, seeing that her eyes were a little misty, but damn, she was a strong woman.

"Your head," she said. "How many stitches, and what did the doctor say?"

"He said it's a scratch and I'm fine. I let him put a couple stitches in."

Jack and Karen were standing just down the hall, talking with Brady and Rosemary. He didn't see Luke, though.

"And what about Charlotte?" Raymond said. "Any news? Is she okay? Was she hurt in the accident?" He looked right at Owen, who just shook his head, then down at Iris.

"We haven't heard anything," Owen said. "We haven't seen Marcus, either. We don't know anything."

"I'll see if I can find out," Raymond said, then squeezed Iris's hand before striding down the hall.

Karen saw him first. "Are you okay?" she said. "Your head…"

He stopped her and slid his arm around her shoulder to hug her. "My head's fine. It's just a scratch. So no one has heard anything? Heard it's a boy, but any news on mother and son, how they're doing?"

Jack shook his head.

Raymond wasn't sure what to make of Brady's expression when he said, "Are you coming back to the house?"

He still had his arm around Karen, holding her and squeezing, knowing what she'd just been through. "We all are," he said. "We're just going to find out first about Charlotte and the baby, and then we're all going home." He took them all in, looking down at Karen. "You talk to your mom?"

Karen shook her head. "There's too much going on right now. Another day."

He rubbed her arm, holding her beside him. He knew Brady didn't have a clue what was going on, by the way he frowned. Rosemary was standing there as well, so quiet, and he thought she was feeling out of place.

"Go sit with your mom, at least, but don't wait too long to talk to her," he added. Then he took in Ryan leaning against the wall, next to Alison, who was sitting on a bench. It looked like Ryan was trying to talk to her. Of course, she was freaked out. He was too, because there had been a moment when he was sure she wasn't going to make it out of that car. How Luke had pulled her out, he didn't know.

"I'm going to talk to Alison," he said, then gave Karen one last hug and rested his hand on Brady's shoulder as he went to walk around him. He paused for a second, taking in his son, who was a man, even though he was still so young. He ran his hand over his son's dark hair, which was just covering his ears, and rustled it. "You need a haircut," he said.

There it was, the tug of his lips, the smile.

Raymond walked away, over to Ryan, who was hovering over Alison, still freaked out. Yeah, that had been way too close. Her expression wasn't the same one he recognized, with that teenage chip on her shoulder that seemed to be part of her prickly personality.

"I heard we still have no news, but it's a boy," Raymond said.

Ryan only nodded. "Yeah, heard from one of the EMTs that they delivered in the back of the ambulance. He didn't say anything else, though, so I don't know how Charlotte is, or the baby. I texted Marcus, but nothing yet. He knows we're down here, waiting. He'll come." Ryan's arms were crossed as he leaned against the wall, and he dragged in a heavy breath. "I'm going to call your mom again," he said, then rested his hand on Alison's shoulder. When she looked up to her dad, he could see the bleakness, likely shock. She only nodded.

"Hey, I'll sit with her," he said, then stepped over and sat down on the bench beside her.

Ryan hesitated only a second before he stepped away. Luke was walking their way now. Where he'd been, Raymond had no idea, but he was heading right for Ryan. They'd have to work it out, this situation with Rosemary. He didn't pull his gaze for a second, long enough to see that at least they were talking.

"You doing okay?" he said.

Alison only shrugged and looked straight ahead. He could see she was looking at Brady.

"It's okay to be freaked out over what happened," he said. "Sometimes talking about it helps. I'm sorry I put us in the ditch." His hands were folded in his lap, and his arm was pressed against hers. She was playing with the rings on her fingers.

"It's not your fault," she said. "That semi came right at us. I thought we were dead."

"I steered the best I could, but you're right: A car and a semi in a head-on isn't a good outcome. But we're here, and we're okay…"

She turned, looking right up at him, and he had to remind himself she was his granddaughter, Ryan's daughter. "What about Charlotte?" she said. "We still haven't heard anything, and the baby? Is Marcus angry at me?"

"No, of course not." He slid his arm around Alison and pulled her closer. "Why would you think that?"

"Because he asked me to look after her, and look what happened. I didn't think we'd get out. I thought I was going to die. Luke…"

He could feel her trembling, and he held her tight, picturing that scene again, how Luke had pulled her out just as the car went over, landing in the snowy ditch with Alison on top of him. Iris had yelled, and then Ryan, everyone down there in that ditch, helping them up, hearing Alison crying.

"Yup, he's a good one to have in a sticky situation. He thinks fast on his feet. And you didn't die, because you're right here, so don't let your head go there. I never got a chance to really talk to you about how you are since everything, Brady, that night…" He knew she understood the night he was referring to, with the guns to their heads as they waited for him, tied up.

She shrugged.

"I put you both through the ringer and never really got to say how sorry I am," he said. "You know, sometimes us adults do some pretty stupid things when we're thinking we're doing the best thing for our families. We're fallible. I'm fallible."

She knit her brows. "Is that an apology? Because it sucks."

He pulled in a breath and took in this precocious kid. No, she wasn't a kid; she was a teenager, a young woman. "Yeah, you're right, it does," he said. "But it wasn't an apology. I just want you to know, even with my best intentions, sometimes I make mistakes. And you and Brady, that was my biggest regret, how you two kids were hurt. He's my son, and you're my granddaughter, and that comes with some pretty big responsibilities I don't take lightly. Just so you know, there isn't a chance Marcus is angry at you. You stuck in the back with Charlotte. You didn't leave her. So don't blame yourself for any of that. You made it out, we all made it out…"

He spotted Marcus coming their way, though he stopped first at Ryan and Luke. Whatever he said, he was smiling, and all of them were hugging, Ryan and then Luke.

"Hey, look." He rubbed Alison's shoulder, and they both stood up.

Karen and Rosemary, Jack, Brady, Owen, and Iris all must have seen Marcus coming, as they walked over.

"We had a boy," Marcus said. "He's doing well, and so is Charlotte."

He heard Owen laugh and call out something, and Karen hugged Marcus, Jack patted his back, and Iris started crying. Raymond rubbed Alison's shoulder as he reached for Iris, putting an arm around her, pulling her closer with Alison beside him, one on each side.

"Was she hurt in the accident, and the baby?" Iris asked.

Marcus shook his head. "She's good, not even a scratch. She's resting upstairs. The doctor said tomorrow she can go home. He's big, eight pounds, two ounces."

"I want to see them. Can we go up?" Iris said. Raymond just rubbed her arm as Marcus nodded.

"Yeah, Mom. Charlotte was asking about you. She was worried you were hurt. I told her everyone was okay, but I think it would do her good to see you all."

Iris pressed her hand to his chest. "I'm going up," she said. "Are you coming? I want to see my grandbaby."

He took in Marcus, who lingered, and then Luke and Rosemary, who were off to the side. Marcus strode over to them.

"Just give me a minute," he said. "I want to talk to Marcus. How about I meet you up there?" He turned to Alison. "Go with your grandma. Go see Charlotte."

Iris reached for her hand and slid her arm around her shoulders.

Raymond glanced over to Owen, Ryan, Brady, Jack, and Karen, who were all walking to the elevator to go up. Then he took one step and then another over to Marcus, Luke, and Rosemary.

"Just wanted to say thanks, Luke," Marcus was saying. "I know I took your head off on the phone…"

Raymond crossed his arms, taking in Marcus and Luke, seeing how uncomfortable Rosemary was. "This was quite the way for you to meet the family," he said. "I never got a chance to say anything, Rosemary, but I'm glad you came. I know you mean a lot to Luke."

She only nodded, and he dragged his gaze over to Luke, seeing the distance between the brothers.

"Don't worry about it, Marcus," Luke said. "It's all good. Just go take care of that wife of yours, and the baby. Rosemary and I are going to slip out, I think."

He wasn't sure for a second what Marcus was going to say as he looked down at Rosemary and then back to Luke.

"Well, we'll be home tomorrow. We'll see you then," Marcus said—to both of them.

Raymond didn't miss the hesitation between Luke and Rosemary as he reached for her hand and then reached out with his other to slap Marcus's shoulder.

"Sure, we'll talk tomorrow," he said. "Give Charlotte a kiss, and that baby too."

Then Luke and Rosemary walked away, and Marcus blew out a breath and shook his head. Raymond could see the tension.

"Well, you know who she is?" Marcus said.

Raymond rested his hand on his son's shoulder. "Yeah, she's the woman your brother fell in love with," he said. "Make sure you understand that. So do you have a name for the baby yet?" He was walking with Marcus to the elevator.

Marcus gave him a tired smile, and he could see the joy in his expression, being a first-time father. "Cameron," he said. "What do you think?"

He squeezed Marcus's shoulder. "Cameron O'Connell...has a nice ring to it."

The elevator doors opened, and Marcus stepped in first, and Raymond hesitated only a second before stepping in behind him.

"Marcus, I'm sorry about the accident," he said. "I never..."

"Hey, don't apologize. If it wasn't for your quick thinking, it could have been much worse. Everyone's fine, my wife, my baby, Mom, Alison. So thank you...Jake." He didn't miss the pull of Marcus's lips.

"Glad you've got it. Now I just have to make sure everyone else is on the same page."

Marcus pressed the button and glanced up to the mirror that security would be watching in the corner. "Of course," he said. "Don't worry, we'll get it. So how long will you and Mom be staying?"

The elevator doors slid open.

"Oh, you know," Raymond said, "until she's convinced every one of you is fine and she's had time to fuss over the baby. Then we'll be on our way."

"So that long, huh?"

He just shook his head, taking in Marcus, who knew his mom so well. "Afraid so," he said.

They stepped out of the elevator, and he spotted his family down the hall and could hear laughter coming from the room.

Yeah, it was likely going to be a little longer.

Marcus's cell phone was ringing, and he took in the number of the sheriff's office before pressing the green answer button. "This is Marcus."

It was on speaker. He glanced once to Charlotte, who was in the passenger seat. Their baby, his son, Cameron, was bundled up and tucked in the back seat. He was bringing them both home from the hospital.

He knew Charlotte was tired and needed some rest, but he also knew his family was waiting at his house. With the excitement of a new O'Connell, even Charlotte wasn't about to tell them not to be there.

"Marcus, it's Colby. There's a Therese Ambrose here. She said she's the new dispatcher."

He grabbed the phone and picked it up, taking it off speaker. Charlotte was staring at him, and he didn't miss the open question there. He put the phone to his ear as he drove the last block home. Colby was still talking.

"She's there now?" Marcus said. What the hell was he

supposed to say, with Charlotte sitting right there, listening to every word?

"Yeah, said she was told to start this morning, but you didn't say anything."

"Listen, I just picked up Charlotte and the baby from the hospital and am bringing them home. Just show her the ropes so she can get started. Consider yourself assigned to babysitting her for the day."

He didn't dare look over to Charlotte even though he could feel her gaze burning into him, considering this was a fact he hadn't shared with her, not entirely. He'd received an email the night before, first congratulating him, then telling him the city council had hired a new dispatcher to take over Charlotte's job.

"Well, do you want me to show her everything Charlotte does? Because I have to tell you, I know how particular Charlotte is about the files, and there are many things I've learned not to touch when it comes to where she keeps things and how the office is run."

Okay, he wasn't talking about this now.

"You know what? Just show her the phones. That's all today. I'll be in later," he said, then hung up before Colby could say anything else.

He glanced at Charlotte as he spotted all the cars outside his house. Smoke rose from the chimney. Evidently, someone had started a fire. He backed into the driveway to make it easier for his wife to get out.

"So you want to explain what that was about?" Charlotte said. "I don't remember ever seeing you grab a phone so quickly, and you took it off speaker so I couldn't hear anything. Someone has been hired to fill in for me? Tell me about this…Therese, is that her name? I should call her and go over a few things."

Marcus turned off the car, knowing Charlotte wasn't

going to take this well, considering he still couldn't believe anyone on the council had thought they could simply replace a woman and take her job because she had a baby.

"We're home," he said. "Do we have to talk about it now? It's cold. Let's go in. And you don't need to call her and talk; Colby can sit with her and show her how to answer the phone. You just had a baby, and you were in an accident yesterday."

There it was: the look, the way she narrowed her eyes. "Marcus O'Connell, you're trying to blow me off by not answering, then telling me you don't want me to talk to someone about how to do my job? I'm no fool. It seems there's something in the works that I don't know about and you do, and you're going to tell me. So what is it? Because I know you, and I don't remember you ever treating me as if I was fragile and didn't have a mind of my own. I may have had a baby, and yes, there was an accident, but we all made it out. I assure you I can think quite clearly, and right now, you have that guilty look as if you've done something. Have you done something?"

He groaned and pulled his hand over his face, then shook his head, pulling the keys from the ignition. "I've done nothing," he said. "I was sent an email because the council took it upon themselves to hire someone for your position without talking to me."

She only shrugged, and he could see she didn't get it. He glanced past her to the door. Owen was walking their way, a smile on his face—a welcome distraction.

He jutted his chin toward him. "There's Owen. The family's here. Let's go in."

Charlotte turned her head, her smile bright as she lifted her hand and opened her door.

"Hey there, little mama. Can I carry anything in?" Owen had Charlotte's door as she unfastened her seatbelt.

"Just the bag in the back. Marcus, you have Cameron?"

He stepped out of the vehicle as Owen helped Charlotte, and he opened the back door and reached in to lift out the car seat, still amazed at how tiny his son was. Cameron was sound asleep, without a care in the world, bundled up with a blanket over him. He walked around the vehicle with the carrier, seeing Owen with Charlotte's bag over his shoulder and his hand on her elbow as she walked. He could see someone had cleared the snow and tossed down some salt for the ice.

The front door squeaked open, and he could hear the voices of his family. It seemed everyone was there, and Charlotte was now inside, being fussed over. The baby carrier was taken from him as soon as he stepped inside the house. His mom, Alison, Suzanne, Jenny, and Eva had the baby in the living room and already out of the carrier. He could hear his brothers in the kitchen and felt the happy vibe in the air. Owen was already pulling off Charlotte's coat, and then he smacked his hand over Marcus's chest.

"Congrats again, baby daddy. So how does it feel to know you're entirely responsible for someone other than yourself?"

He knew Owen was teasing, but there was something about watching his mom holding his baby and everyone around her fussing. He felt a weight that he hadn't felt before. He wondered if that was why he'd woken up at four a.m. in a cold sweat, his heart hammering, because of the little life he was now responsible for.

"If you're trying to scare me, you're too late," Marcus said. "Charlotte, you want to go upstairs and lie down and get some sleep?"

She was shaking her head as she sat on the stairs and pulled off her shoes, wearing matching cream-colored sweats and a sweatshirt. She lifted her gaze to him and then dragged it over to Owen. "Did you know that Marcus is keeping another secret?"

Owen stilled, alarm on his face, before he dragged his gaze over to Marcus. "You are?" he said.

Marcus could hear the hum of conversation in the background, his family. "Ah, Charlotte…"

She lifted a brow. "Yes, it seems he doesn't want to tell me about a new person who's taking over my job. Someone is needed to fill in for me while I'm home with the baby, yet I can tell when Marcus is hiding something. You know, he changes the subject and acts kind of the way he is right now."

Evidently, she wasn't going to let it go.

"What's going on here?" Karen said, taking in Charlotte. "Hey, you. So glad you're okay and home." She gave Charlotte's hand a squeeze. She was dressed in black track pants and wool socks, with a white V-neck knit overtop. He wondered how his sister was doing, considering she was having to put on a brave face.

"I'm being cornered," Marcus said.

"No, Marcus," Charlotte said. "I may just have had a baby, but I know when you're evading, and you are." She slid her gaze over to Karen. "Just before we pulled in, Colby phoned and told him a woman showed up to fill in for me. Therese, was it?" She glanced over and up to Marcus from where she sat on the stairs, and he wasn't sure whether he was supposed to answer.

She pulled her gaze away, looking at Owen first and then back to Karen, as she continued: "I've never seen Marcus take a phone off speaker so fast, especially while driving. Why he wouldn't want me to hear is a mystery to me. When I asked, Marcus, what did you say, exactly? Something along the lines of us being home and not having to talk about it now, so of course I know something's up."

Owen's expression was amused as Marcus dragged his gaze from him to Charlotte.

Karen, meanwhile, was glaring daggers his way. "So this is just a temp you've brought in, right?" she said.

Marcus now found himself in the line of fire, with three pairs of eyes staring at him, pinning him to the spot. He rested an arm on the railing and leaned against it as he considered how to answer, well aware that there were two versions of Karen, sister and lawyer. Which one was asking now, he wasn't sure.

"No," was all he got out, because Karen was already staring at him with the kind of look he couldn't remember her ever directing at him.

"What's going on here?" Jack said, walking their way, wearing a navy lightweight knit and blue jeans, holding a coffee.

Karen still hadn't pulled her gaze from him. "Are you telling me you've given Charlotte's job away to someone else?"

Charlotte seemed to be comfortable letting Karen speak for her, and Marcus wasn't sure, by Jack's expression, whether he was going to jump in to his defense.

"Not me," he said. "I had no say. I was sent an email that the council had hired someone for Charlotte's position…"

"And you promptly emailed them back, citing labor relations laws that state you can't take away a woman's job because she's had a baby," Karen said. She was on a roll now, and she even jabbed a finger at Charlotte and said, "I'll handle this."

Jenny was now walking over too, holding the baby, with his mom, likely to see what was going on. He could see his dad and Ryan talking in the living room and wondered if they too would be joining this interrogation.

"No," Marcus said, "because I was getting ready to pick up Charlotte from the hospital. Since I'm already in the doghouse, I may as well tell you that I was called in to meet with the council a few days ago and was told that Charlotte's job would be given to someone who needed it, as they expected she'd be staying home with the baby."

He wasn't sure if everyone's expressions were of disbelief or shock. In the quiet that lingered for a second, he could actually hear his dad and Ryan talking, and he thought he heard Eva and Alison in the kitchen.

"Someone on the council took away Charlotte's job and gave it to someone else because she had a baby?" Suzanne said, jumping in.

He hadn't realized she was there, and he found himself dragging his hand over his face and down.

"Who, Marcus?" she said. "Who would do that? They're aware that it's completely illegal, right?"

He thought he groaned. He wished the baby would cry right about now. "You know what? I'd rather not say…"

Karen raised a brow. "Well, I'm sorry, but I'm going to insist you start talking."

Even Jack gave him the kind of look that said, *Dude, seriously?*

Owen reached over and smacked him on the arm lightly. "Even I know that's a no-go zone," he said. "Stop protecting whoever it is, considering Karen is likely ready to march down to City Hall and start demanding. You may as well toss the dirtbag under the bus, unless…"

"Unless what?" he snapped, feeling very much under attack. The hurt in Charlotte's expression was the thing that bothered him most about all this, as he'd never wanted her to know.

"Unless it was your idea…" Owen said. In the silence after, he swore, and Jack too. Jenny and his mom started in, as well, and he found himself lifting his hand because everyone was talking.

"Okay, this is ridiculous," he said. "It was absolutely not my idea, and I was honestly furious when I first heard it, sitting before the council—which, I might also point out, I'm still treading water with, as they would prefer I weren't sheriff. Regardless, it was put out there by Jessa, who evidently had the support of the council and the mayor. The email last night said they had hired someone for Charlotte's job, not temporarily but permanently. To make it worse, someone on the council clearly knows they've broken all kinds of labor laws here, because the email emphasized that she's a minority and ticks every box: She's a woman, a single mother who put herself through school at night and comes from one of the poorer families around, and she's black. Yes, that was in the email, word for word."

No one said anything. From the shock on Charlotte's face, and Karen's too, he wondered what they'd add.

"So, you see, someone has put some thought into this," he said.

"Right, because fighting to get Charlotte her job back could suddenly become a race issue," Jack said. "You'd be seen as opportunistic. That's deviously smart."

"So, basically, what you're saying is that the council not only screwed me but would be forcing me to screw her if I try to get my job back," Charlotte said.

Karen let out a heavy sigh.

"Dirty, dirty…" Suzanne said as she turned away. "My turn to hold the baby."

He stood there until it was just him and Charlotte and Owen left, and he dragged his gaze down to Charlotte.

"You tell me what you want to do, and you know I'm a hundred percent behind you. I already said my piece and called them out, saying there was no way in hell they could give your job away, but my voice isn't being heard. You want to fight it?"

She was already shaking her head as she rested her hand on the railing and stood up. "Let me think on it, Marcus. You know I love my job," she said, then started walking into the living room, where everyone was fussing over the baby. That left just him and Owen, who was still shaking his head.

"That's a bad spot to be in. Wouldn't want to be you right now. Doesn't matter what way you look at it; one of these women is getting screwed." Owen patted his shoulder again and went to walk away.

"Hey, listen," Marcus said. "With all the excitement, I never asked you about that family. Did you decide to take a chance and work on some arrangement to let them stay in your house?"

Owen glanced over his shoulder into the living room. There was nothing amused in his expression as he crossed his arms. "Yeah, I got down there to the camp, and you were right. It got to me, seeing how down and out everyone was, having to live like that. But to answer your question, I didn't end up offering my house to that family. I met them and talked with them, but I offered it to a single woman there instead."

He wasn't sure what to say and even lifted his hand. "I don't understand. Why wouldn't you have helped that family?"

Owen shrugged. "They'll be okay. They'll find something, because people will always take a chance on a family with two parents, a man and a woman, with kids. That's more than anyone else there has. It bothered me that everyone was overlooking that woman. I saw her there, and I walked over and asked her story. She's forty-seven but looks like an old woman. Life on the streets hasn't been kind. She's spent half her life there, been beat up, robbed, raped. She aged out of the system when she was eighteen and was forced to live on the streets. She's had jobs and a roof over her head before. The last one was subsidized housing, but it was bought by a developer. Remember that one outside downtown, the rundown shithole that took substandard to another level? Well, when it was bought, everyone who lived there was evicted, and she found herself back on the streets, while the building was torn down and turned into condos that sold at a premium.

"So no, I didn't rent my place to that family, because as rough as it is for them, it was worse for Brandy—which is her name, by the way. Seeing the bleakness, the fact that she's spent most of her life just surviving, I rented her my place on the condition that she look after it. She'll do some work in my home office, answering phones, whatever, to help with my plumbing business." Owen tapped his chest with the back of his hand. "I'm surprised at you, Marcus. You, out of everyone, should know that as hard as it is on the streets for everyone, for women, it's ten times harder. With everything that happened to her, she knew there was no justice coming to help her."

As his brother walked away, Marcus suddenly felt shame. He'd had blinders on, seeing only that family, rather than everyone else in the camp, as people worthy of help.

Eighteen

"So is the baby asleep?" Karen said.

Marcus had pulled on a dark blue shirt, his sheriff's badge pinned to it. His duty belt, minus the gun, which she knew he kept locked in a gun safe upstairs, was resting on the table at the front door. "Yeah, Mom put him down. Not a peep out of him. He's in a bassinet beside our bed. Mom insisted Charlotte sleep. I know she's happy Mom is here, and even though I suggested she go to bed and get some rest, Mom telling her to sleep when the baby does was all it took."

Karen could hear voices from the kitchen, the spot everyone seemed to gather. Ryan had left because he had to go to work, and so had Tessa, because school was in session. Jenny, too, had packed up Eva and Alison and taken them to school for a late check-in. "Well, then we should probably clear out," she said.

Marcus was shaking his head as he sat in the easy chair across from where Karen was sitting alone on the sofa, having slipped away from everyone to give herself a minute to settle her thoughts. "No," he said. "Another thing Mom said was that we shouldn't tiptoe around the baby or every sound will wake him. Charlotte, I think, finds it comforting to know you're all here downstairs."

She heard footsteps on the stairs and took in her mom, content, happy, dressed in blue jeans and a simple light blue knit sweater, and her dad was with her. Seeing them together now, she could tell how much they loved each other. Going all those years without being together, she didn't know how her mom had done it. Her dad was talking and glanced over to her, and she knew he was saying something about her, so she looked back over to Marcus, who seemed to be stuck in some heavy thoughts.

"Sorry if I came down on you, Marcus," she said, "but you have to know that laws have actually been passed to prevent employers from doing exactly what the council just did, taking away a woman's job because she had a baby or is pregnant. Should I go on?"

Marcus lifted his gaze to her, and she could see how tired he was, how pissed off. He was ready to argue and give it right back. "You think I don't know that?" he said. "That's why I said nothing. You have any idea what it was like for me, having to hear the council talking about getting rid of my wife? It was dirty, how they went about it, and underhanded. And if we fight it, who do you think is going to look bad? I guarantee you Charlotte and I will come out looking opportunistic, and if it comes to a fight, Charlotte's character will come under attack, and the events of the past few months will get brought up again."

"It's not right, Marcus," Karen said.

"I know that," he snapped, then pulled in a breath as if realizing how sharply it had come out. "Sure, she can fight, and you too. I know you'd love to get your hands into this, but now there's another woman in the mix, and she didn't ask for any of this. She's being played like a puppet by the city council."

"You mean Therese, the lady hired to replace Charlotte?"

He didn't nod. "You're a smart, successful woman, Karen. How many times have you had to fight against the kind of underhandedness you'd never have to face if you were a man? The character attacks, maybe threats, because you're seen as defenseless?"

She couldn't believe her brother got it or had even seen it. "Too many times," she said. "Didn't think you knew."

He shrugged. "I hear about it. Don't often see it, because it wouldn't happen to me, and when I walk into a room, it suddenly stops. But I do remember how it was for Mom. Being a kid on the sidelines, watching, listening, I saw some things I've never forgotten—the way she was talked to and treated at times. Yeah, I know. Maybe that's why I'm having trouble with this. Would it be easier for Charlotte to just stay home and not fight this? It would, of course. It seems the writing is on the wall that the council is working behind the scenes to find a way to get rid of me, and I'm very aware that they did what they did because Charlotte is my wife. So how about we table this discussion? I don't want to talk about it any more today. Let's talk about you and how you're doing. I know you didn't tell anyone, but I also know you weren't in there, fighting with everyone to hold the baby. You okay being here?"

She didn't know why, but she glanced over to her mom, who was giving everything to her as her dad talked. From the expression on her face, Karen knew her dad was telling her about her losing the baby.

"I'm good," she finally said. "It's a shitty thing, you know, but one day at a time…"

Her mom was there now, walking into the room.

Marcus cleared his throat and stood up. "Well, I actually have to get into the office, so I'm going to leave all of you here," he said, then hesitated only a second, touching his mom's shoulder, before walking around behind Karen and resting his hand on her shoulder, too.

As she looked up, she felt the gentle touch and saw his support for her.

"You need anything, you call," was all he said before walking away.

Her mom was looking at her closely now, and she pulled in a breath and sat down beside her on the sofa, reaching over to rest her hand on her leg. "You should have told me," she said.

Karen glanced over, taking in her dad, who was now at the door, talking to Marcus. "I'm sorry. I wasn't planning on telling anyone…"

Her mom only nodded, and for a moment, she wondered if her mom was hurt.

"Jack called Dad, and…"

Her mom squeezed her leg gently and then linked their fingers together. "Your dad just told me. I'm glad he went to see you. You and your dad always had this relationship that no one else in the family had, so I'm not surprised, but at the same time, I'm so sorry."

She only nodded and turned back to her mom beside her. "Dad said you lost two babies. How come you never said anything?" she asked. Looking at her, Karen couldn't remember a time her mom hadn't been there for all of them. Her dad had left, but her mom had been there.

"It's not something I wanted to talk about," Iris said. "Having all of you, I didn't have the luxury of wallowing. Yes, it was hard, but your dad was there, even though I pushed him away for a bit when it happened. He seemed to understand, I think, as he did more with you kids for a bit. Then I just pushed on, because that's what you do, but you don't forget. I didn't forget. Your dad, he was there for me and knew how much it hurt me. At the same time, he never let on that he was hurting, too—just like your Jack. You know, even though your dad wasn't the one who lost the baby, it was still his loss, and it took me a long time to see that. The same goes for your Jack, so don't shut him out."

The way her mom said it, she wondered if she knew how she'd pushed him away, how he hadn't left even when she tried to make him. "But he can't understand how I feel…"

Her mom squeezed her hand. "No one can. That's why you have to tell him how you feel and let him in. You'll mourn for a bit, wondering what if, and why. I had to remind myself I had all of you. You and Jack will get past this. You'll try again. It's okay to be sad for a bit, but those thoughts that you did something… There isn't a woman out there who doesn't somehow, on some level, think she did something, but you didn't. It just happens, and it's shitty."

"So is this your idea of a pep talk?"

A soft smile touched her mom's lips as she leaned back on the sofa, just sitting with Karen, holding her hand, and looking at their linked fingers. "There's no sugar-coating this. I'm not going to give you a pep talk, so to speak, because there's no way to make light of this. It happened, and I'm sorry, but as you know well, sometimes life does things to you that make you wonder about the fairness of it. But you have us, all of us."

That was all her mom said as they sat there together, alone, in the kind of comfortable silence she wanted right now.

"You know, I didn't want to admit how much I wanted

this baby," she said. As she turned to her mom, she saw her gaze filled with an understanding she hadn't expected, and she just nodded and smiled softly again.

"I know you did. Come here," Iris said, and she let go of her hand and slid her arm around her shoulder to pull her against her.

Karen pressed her hand to her face when tears she'd never expected to shed came out of nowhere.

CHAPTER
Nineteen

"You're really good with him, you know?" Rosemary said.

He was driving her Jeep, considering his pickup had been parked at the airport since he'd flown to Indiana, where he'd convinced her it was time to meet his family and had offered to drive them both back.

The excitement that had been there was long gone now, though, as he took in the high school they were idling in front of. He'd just dropped Brady off for his math class, even though he'd argued that he didn't want or need to go. Beside him, Rosemary couldn't hide the distance she'd put up around herself.

"He's family," was his only response. Where did he and Rosemary stand now? He was at a loss for what to say to a woman who'd continued to pull away.

"And you're modest," she said. "One of the qualities I like about you is that you don't negotiate with Brady, but you listen to him. He's a good kid, and you have a good family…"

"I sense a 'but' coming." He tapped his hand on the

steering wheel before putting the Jeep in gear and pulling back out into traffic. He'd promised his mom that he'd stop in at Marcus's and see the baby, even though he didn't think showing up with Rosemary again was a great idea.

"I really, really care about you, Luke, more than I wanted to admit—more than I wanted to allow myself," she said. "But I'm afraid if I let this thing continue for us, you could end up losing some of your family, and I don't want to be responsible for you having to choose."

He said nothing. He'd never expected the backlash he'd received, but then, he'd never planned on telling his family who Rosemary's brother was, because, in his mind, it wasn't relevant.

"You know what I do," he said. It wasn't a question, and he could feel her watching him.

"Yes, Luke. That's how we met, remember. Your point?" she replied with a ton of sarcasm, just something else he loved about her.

"Then you know I've made a lot of enemies. Look, what we were ordered to do, securing your dad because someone in our government didn't want him exposing a fraud and the fact that our government was actually hurting people… Your brothers came after us. You came after us. You know I can't talk about what I have to do, because it's classified and falls under national security, but it falls into a gray area. If made known, it could have some real repercussions."

He glanced over. She was staring out the window.

"I'm waiting for the point you're trying to make," she finally said as she looked over to him, unimpressed.

"The point is that when I come home, I get to be someone else. I step into the role of a good old homeboy who protects his country, kind of like a hero, of sorts, yet no one really wants to know the details of what I do. If they did, you think I'd be welcome?"

She said nothing at first. Then, "You joined the military to protect your country."

"Yet it's not just about terrorism anymore. We seem to be protecting corporate greed more and more, but no one seems to get that. You seem to be okay with my family holding you responsible for what your brother did—even though you're not your brother, and I don't know how many ways I can tell you that until you believe it—but I know that what I've had to do, in their minds, would be worse."

She slid her gaze over to him. "You sound like your dad."

He wasn't sure what to make of that.

She pulled in a breath and let it out. "If that's your way of trying to convince me to stay, that it will work out, then I disagree," she said. "I don't want to feel as if I'm the enemy. I know very well how much your family cares about you, but at the same time, Luke, they asked you to go because of me, to leave your brother's house and take me. The hate I saw in your brothers' eyes for me…" She stopped talking and shook her head, and he found himself squeezing the wheel a little harder before she continued, saying, "I told your dad the same thing."

"Whoa, wait a second. What do you mean, you told my dad? When did you talk to him?"

The snow on the roadside had recently been plowed, and he felt the give under his tires, the slickness on the roads. Winter driving conditions were here.

"When you were in the shower this morning," she said. "I was reading the paper in the living room, and your dad brought me a coffee and sat down and joined me. Nice man. He said exactly what you said, asked me to give your siblings some time, saying that they would come around because you're family, and that's what family does. He asked me not to take responsibility for something I didn't do. He asked me, too, how I felt about you. Can't remember ever feeling so uncomfortable or on the spot as I did during that little talk."

She said nothing else as he turned the corner, getting closer to Marcus's and seeing Ryan pass in his ranger's pickup. He honked and lifted his hand in a wave.

"Well…?" he added, tossing Rosemary another glance.

She looked away, and he couldn't figure out what she was thinking as they pulled up in front of Marcus's house, seeing smoke from the chimney, his family's cars parked outside. He turned off the engine and sat there with her before she finally pulled in a breath, reached for her seatbelt, and unbuckled it.

"I said I could see the kind of forever with you that wasn't possible," she said, and that had his heart sinking. "I really care about you, Luke, and I think you know that, but the minute I walked into your brother's house with you and saw that little girl and knew how frightened she would've been, and when I opened my mouth and told your brothers who I was, I knew we could never have that happily ever after. That can't happen for people like us. What you do, what I did, what my brother did, there are consequences, and although maybe your family will come around, maybe I don't want the reminder of what my brother almost did and who he became. Maybe I shouldn't have said anything, but there was something about standing there with your family. I felt myself in the middle of a lie. My dad is forever in hiding, and there can't be a clean slate here, not in my mind. Your dad didn't agree, but I think he saw I had my mind made up, even though he did his best to persuade me otherwise for you. He really loves you, all of you."

He wasn't sure what to say to that. "So this is it?" he finally said as he took in the front door opening. Marcus stood there, and Rosemary looked over to him.

"Yeah, it's better this way," she said. "I'll just go. I hope you find someone, Luke. You have a nice family, but…" She shook her head, and he didn't miss how red her eyes were. She forced a smile. "While the sun is out, I should get going. It's a long drive."

"You should stay a day or two for the roads to clear. I can drive you back…"

She was shaking her head. "I'm a big girl, Luke, and I've driven in worse. I'll be careful."

He knew that was his cue, and he had known as soon as he saw Marcus step out of the house that he couldn't linger anymore, so he opened the door.

Rosemary slipped around the stick shift into the driver's seat. Her suitcase was already in the back, where she'd put it. Evidently, she'd made her mind up, and there was no changing it, no matter what.

He stood there in the open door as she started the Jeep, taking in her image, her lips, which he'd lost count of how many times he'd kissed. He'd touched her, loved her. He leaned in and kissed her briefly, then pulled back.

"Drive safe," he said, and he stopped himself from saying one more thing—*I'll call you. I'll see you again.*

She only nodded as she reached for the door and pulled it closed, and he stepped back as she pulled out into the street.

Marcus was on the sidewalk now, taking in her Jeep driving away. He looked over to him. "Was that Rosemary leaving?"

He started up the walkway. "Yeah, she's heading back

to Indiana," he replied, and he wasn't sure, by the expression on his brother's face, what he was going to say.

"Because of us?" he finally said.

Luke took in the house, knowing his family was inside. "Because of what happened, mostly. Seeing what her brother almost did, she's having a hard time not believing she's guilty by relation. She wasn't responsible for it, and remember, I was the one who killed him. You never asked, not that I'd tell you, what I did to bring that trouble here."

Marcus glanced away, narrowing his gaze. He was likely still conflicted, thinking. Then he nodded. "It's the reminder, Luke. I know she's not her brother, but at the same time…knowing who she is would be a reminder—and I'm not sure I want to know what you had to do, even if you could say. Would you like me to apologize for my part in chasing her away?"

He wondered for a moment whether Marcus meant it. He shook his head. "No, I don't think it would matter at this point. It seems that maybe it was doomed from the beginning with Rosemary. She's not willing, and I'm…well, out of arguments. Are you off to work?"

Marcus gave everything to him. "Yeah, some problems to deal with. Most everyone's inside." He jutted his chin toward the house, his breath misting in the winter cold, then started to his sheriff's car, which was parked and covered with snow.

Luke was already walking to the house when Marcus called out to him. He turned and waited for a second.

"We would have come around, you know, for you," Marcus said.

Luke glanced up the road, no longer seeing Rosemary's Jeep. "Go deal with what you need to deal with," he said, then turned and strode up the steps.

Hearing the voices of his family inside, he realized the

things he did and who he was made it impossible for him to have a typical relationship. He'd tried to pretend Rosemary could fit into his life, but as he looked back to his brother, who was sweeping the snow off his vehicle, he realized he wasn't about to walk away from his family, not for anyone.

Rosemary may have been right about that—but she was wrong about his family. They would have come around. They would have done it for him

Turn the page for a sneak peek of
AND THEN SHE WAS GONE coming next in *THE O'CONNELLS*
Available in print, eBook & Audio

The moment Brady told his family he was engaged, his fiancée was nowhere to be found.

Six months ago, Brady's true love, Cassie Arnold, walked into his hometown and his life. Everything was perfect, including their plans for their upcoming wedding—but one night, when he came home, Cassie was gone.

How could she just vanish?

Brady turns to his sheriff brother, Marcus O'Connell, and is stunned by what he discovers. Not only is there no trace of her, but it's as if she never existed.

As they dig deeper into the days before Cassie vanished, Brady is stunned to learn of a series of mysterious phone calls, and he realizes his bride-to-be and her seemingly perfect smile were hiding dark secrets, including an unsolved murder at her family's cabin in a hometown he's never heard of.

Brady soon suspects that to find Cassie, he may also have to figure out what really happened the night of the murder—and why Cassie kept it all a secret.

And Then She Was Gone

CHAPTER 1

How was it possible that Brady had woken up one day and become part of something bigger, something that still didn't seem real?

It was his nineteenth birthday today, and he wasn't sure what to expect as he walked down the street with his hands shoved in his lightweight black down winter jacket. He took in the familiar sidewalk, one he'd walked a hundred times, and the heavy clouds in the darkening sky. The unusual cold predicted an early snow any day.

As he arrived at Marcus's two-storey craftsman, he looked across the street to Ryan's. The two brothers lived in a neighborhood where all the homes were similar. Welcoming light drifted out the living room window. He took a second to look around at the vehicles of his family, reminding himself they weren't strangers. Harold's new KIA, Tessa's older Buick, the sheriff's car his brother drove, and Charlotte's Subaru were all in the driveway.

He breathed out fog. It was cold tonight.

"Hey, birthday boy. What are you doing standing out there? Get your ass in here."

Brady hadn't expected Luke back yet, and although his older-model pickup was nowhere to be seen, there he was, standing in the open door, wearing blue jeans and a faded T-shirt. It seemed he'd packed on even more muscle. He held a beer, sporting the beginnings of a beard, and his shoulder-length hair was hanging loose. So he was letting it grow back out.

"I didn't know you were back," Brady said. And where had he been? No one else asked, but he always did.

"Just got here," Luke said. "You didn't think I'd miss your birthday, did you? Kind of expected you to still be at my mom's place, but you were gone. You walk over?"

Brady stepped up onto the porch, hearing laughter and voices inside. His ears were stinging from the cold. "I stopped for a haircut," he said, though he wished he hadn't. He only ever went to Iris's place to change these days, and he couldn't remember the last time he'd even slept there.

"Short and neat for your birthday, or is it a girl you're trying to impress?" Luke said. "Get in here before you let all the heat out." He ran his hand roughly over Brady's head.

As Brady stepped inside the warm house, he thought of the girl whose smile had him taking a second and third glance in the mirror to check how he looked and how he dressed. "It was time for a cut, you know—but I probably should've asked where not to go."

Luke leaned on the railing, his expression puzzled, eyebrows knit. Amused? He wasn't so sure, but he knew Luke was ready to listen, as always.

"Brady, it's about time you got here," Ryan called out with a smile from the kitchen, the place everyone gathered.

Brady pulled off his coat. Luke was still watching him

with that heavy, patient gaze. He knew Luke had many depths to him.

"So where, pray tell, did you go, and what happened? Give me the scoop." Luke tossed his coat behind him on a chair as Brady kicked off his sneakers, which had seen better days.

"That place across from the diner, at the edge of downtown."

"Not Clarissa's?"

The way his brother said it had him hesitating a second. "Blond, heavyset, cakes the makeup on?"

"That's her, the very same. Let me guess: She pumped you for all the dirt on my mom…"

There it was again, that uncomfortable feeling he'd had the moment he figured out she knew who he was and was getting too familiar with him.

"How'd you know that?" Brady said. "Yeah, she knew who I was and asked about every one of you, then gave me a blow by blow of your entire lives from her perspective, even though I didn't ask."

Then there was the moment the conversation had shifted to Raymond, when she'd said how sorry she was to hear he was dead, and he'd wanted her to hurry the hell up so he could get his ass out of that chair and leave the salon before he said something he knew he couldn't.

"That's why she gets her hair done the county over when she's here," Luke said. "But you look good—almost too pretty." Luke rubbed his hair again roughly, playfully, the way he did too many times, and then had them walking into the kitchen.

Marcus was holding Cameron, who had just started walking. His first birthday was only a month away, around the corner, another big celebration, he was sure. He had dark hair and the O'Connell blue eyes Brady didn't. He wondered if he'd ever feel the close bond that seemed to exist naturally between his other siblings.

"About time you got here, kid. Was about to send out a search party for you," Owen said as he walked over with an open beer and slipped it to him.

Brady stared at it for a second, not missing the twitch of Owen's lips, and he didn't hesitate any further before lifting it to his lips and taking a swallow. "Thanks," he said.

Ryan gave him a smile, and Suzanne rolled her eyes, whereas Marcus angled his head and just shook it. He wondered for a moment whether Marcus would take the beer from him.

"Just FYI, kid, this is a one-time pass," Marcus said, sounding much like his dad. "I'll pretend I'm not seeing it, but one beer only, understand?" He gave a pointed look to Owen.

Alison was keeping to the background, her hair hiked high in a ponytail, her eyes coated with smoky shadow. The auburn shirt she wore was cut low in a V. He only nodded before he had to pull his gaze away. The tension still lingered. He wondered if it always would.

"I see you got a haircut, cleaned yourself up," Ryan said, Jenny leaning against him. "Since dinner isn't ready, we should give you your birthday present early…" His eyes flickered with the sort of teasing his brothers seemed ready and willing to dish out more and more to him as of late.

He heard the back door and spotted Harold, his blond hair in the same cop cut he always wore. The barbecue was smoking out back, and he was wearing only a navy sweater.

"The barbecue is ready. You want me to throw the burgers on?" Harold said, then walked over to him. "Hey, kid, happy birthday. I see we're now encouraging underage drinking."

He knew Harold was teasing, and Suzanne only shook her head from where she was dumping a premade salad into a bowl. She wore a baseball shirt that accentuated her tall, lanky frame.

"He's nineteen, everyone," she said. "He's legal to drink somewhere. And remember when you were sixteen, Marcus and Ryan, what happened to Mom's bottle of vodka?"

There was silence for a second as Marcus slid his gaze to Suzanne. Another layer was being peeled back, another secret. He figured Marcus and Ryan had a bunch of exploits they'd never share.

Suzanne crumpled up the salad bag and tossed it into the recycling bin under the sink. "By the way, Karen texted. She and Jack are coming tonight. Maybe we should hold off on the birthday gifts until they get here?"

Marcus handed a fussing Cameron, who was rubbing his eyes, off to Charlotte. "No, this gift is just from the brothers," he said. "You and Karen can add your gift when she gets here. Come on, Brady."

Marcus had his hand on his shoulder and was steering him into the living room, directing him to Charlotte's rocking chair by the window, and everyone seemed to follow them. Charlotte had gone upstairs, carrying Cameron, whom he could hear crying now, and Eva and Alison had gone with her.

"You got me a gift?" Brady said.

Marcus rested his hands on the back of the sofa and looked over to him, whereas Luke took the easy chair, and Owen sat on the sofa across from him and rested a foot on the coffee table, dressed in the same blue jeans he'd worn at the job site and his usual five o'clock shadow, because shaving was something he did only every few days.

"Yes. Let's start with the fact that words matter,"

Marcus said. "You're nineteen, which puts you squarely in that age category I remember well, where you operate from hot emotion and say the first thing that comes to mind. Your mouth is and will be an issue and can land you in a ton of hot water, so learn to dial it back, way back, so you don't have to wish you could go back and say nothing instead. Think first before you say anything. That will save you from landing in a world of trouble with the kind of words that can't be taken back."

Brady just stared at him before looking over to Jenny and Ryan. The way she looked down on him, he wondered whether he had done or said something he shouldn't have. At the same time, he was still looking for the gift. Had they hidden it? He leaned forward and looked around Luke.

"Okay, fine," he said. "Watch what I say. Got it—but I'm pretty thoughtful, I think…" He lifted the beer and took another swallow, still not believing that Marcus was looking the other way and letting him drink.

"Be a damn good brother," Ryan cut in, gesturing toward him before crossing his arms.

Brady just blinked, wondering what this was. "Okay… check. I didn't think I was a terrible brother. Is there something specific you're getting at in a brotherly way that I've missed? Is this the buildup to the gift?"

Across from him, Owen was giving him everything with that heavy gaze. Tessa sat on the arm of the sofa beside him, her blond hair pulled up in soft, wavy curls that couldn't be tamed. "Your gift is advice from your brothers," Owen said, "so listen up. We're a family. Being the youngest, you didn't grow up with us, so you don't know how things work. You're getting a crash course since you've been with us for only almost a year. Family comes first. If you get a call that your brother has found himself arrested and is in jail, you bail him out, no questions asked. Right, Ryan and Marcus?"

Brady realized he was serious. "What! Wait, one of you got arrested?" he said.

Ryan lifted his beer and shook his head, but the expression on his face said everything. "Yeah, at seventeen. Good thing Mom isn't here. We never told her about it."

He wondered if his eyes bugged out.

Marcus was still leaning on the back of the sofa, shaking his head. Brady was seeing his brother, the sheriff, through completely different eyes these days. Maybe he was human after all. Meanwhile, from the way Suzanne stared, he was pretty sure this was the first she was hearing of the arrest, as well.

"You're serious!" she said. "Holy shit, I never had any idea. Does Karen know?"

Marcus shook his head and let out a rude noise. "No one was supposed to know about it. Remember to take it to your grave. Pretty sure those were your words, Owen."

"Hey, you're the one who had the brilliant idea of setting Brady straight on how we work as a family," Owen said. "At least I haven't shared all your secrets."

Marcus grimaced as he stood up and then pulled a hand over his face. "I sold the '72 Chevy I was rebuilding —I loved that car—to bail your ass out," he said, gesturing to Ryan.

Suzanne was still staring in horror, while Harold seemed amused. Luke and Owen were shaking their heads. It seemed Brady had no idea of the escapades that went on in this family, among his siblings, whom he was still getting to know.

"Yeah, but the only reason I landed in jail was because of you," Ryan said. "I was just the one who got caught holding the spray cans."

"Only because I'm faster," Marcus said. "I could never figure out why the charges suddenly went away. Guess now we know."

"Dad," Ryan said.

"Never got the bail money back, though."

Harold let out a laugh and shook his head as if this wasn't the first time he'd heard something along these lines. Brady wondered at times whether Harold understood the siblings better than he ever would.

"Dad did say he was watching," Suzanne said. "Do you suppose he made sure the charges were dropped and your bail money disappeared to teach you a lesson?"

He spotted headlights outside. Karen, maybe. He missed her, considering she and Jack were now in Missoula, which meant she could no longer stick her nose in every part of his business. He never thought he'd miss that.

"Maybe," Marcus said. "It's likely, since Dad seemed to know the details of what we were doing."

"And what, exactly, were you doing?" Suzanne asked. "You never really answered us, Marcus, when Dad brought it up last year, saying he'd been watching. He mentioned a string of robberies."

Marcus shifted his stance. Brady could see he was uncomfortable in the spotlight. Something seemed to pass between him and Ryan. They really did seem like partners in crime.

"Dad was right: I was a little shit," Marcus said. "But now I'm not. End of story. Let's move on, because this is about Brady."

"He broke into several stores," Owen cut in. "One was to steal the spray paint, and you lifted some parts for the Chevy, stole some camping gear…what else was it?"

Brady looked over to Ryan and then Marcus, who just

cleared his throat. Jenny smacked Ryan's chest, but her amused expression said this was no surprise to her.

"And you knew?" Suzanne said.

Owen made a face and shrugged. "Who do you think helped Marcus get the money for his car and went with him to the cop shop to get Ryan out? You forget how I had to keep an eye on all of you."

"Okay, we're getting off track here," Marcus said. "The point is, Brady, you get yourself in a jam, you call. You don't try to figure it out yourself. We all are your first call, and that makes you ours. If we call you for help in any way, it's no questions asked. You just show up."

Brady wasn't sure what to make of that. On the sofa, Tessa shook her head, and Owen lifted his gaze to her, resting his hand on her thigh.

"Fine, got it," Brady said. "So if I get myself arrested, I'll call you, but seriously, I'm not planning on it."

"That's good," Owen said. "Keep your nose clean, stay out of trouble—"

"And be a damn hard worker," Luke jumped in, cutting Owen off.

"When you believe in something, you stand up for it," Owen said. "You do right by your family, and you know who your family is. We have your back, and it goes both ways. You don't go off half-cocked alone, like Luke," he added, looking over to him.

Luke seemed to be quite comfortable, but he never really knew what his brother was thinking. Maybe he needed to take their advice and check in with Luke, who hadn't let on how he was since splitting with Rosemary. He really did hide what he was thinking.

"Hey," Luke said, gesturing with his beer and taking them all in. "We all need time alone sometimes, but know I'm one call away and always have been. No questions asked, ever. You know that, all of you. Lost count of the jams and scrapes I've found myself in, cleaning up after you all."

"If you're hurting, scared, screwed up, or confused about anything, you come here, to us," Marcus said. "You get stuck in your head at times, Brady, and you wear your heart on your sleeve. That's good sometimes, but others it isn't."

"And you always do your best," Owen said. "There's no shame in doing average hard work, the kind you're doing. You've got a trade under your belt now, and you're set. You finish the job, no complaints."

Brady was working for his brother now in his plumbing business, apprenticing, because he hadn't come up with a better option. That day almost a year ago, before Iris and his dad had left again, Owen had simply pulled up in his plumbing van and said, "Get in!"

"You never gave me a choice," Brady said. "I finished high school and thought of taking a few courses at college, but when I couldn't get in, you said I had to do something instead of sitting around, so you made me carry your tools and watch over your shoulder, crawl into holes, get dirty every day… Have I complained yet?"

Owen didn't seem impressed. His older brother didn't say much but seemed to always have his eye on him, telling him where to go, which job site to be at, and what to do. He wondered when he should start looking for something else, but what? He had no experience and had never worked before, because his dad had always moved him to some new city or state before he could get too comfortable.

"Well, you just make sure you don't start complaining," Owen said. "Anyway, when it comes to family, we stand beside each other, all of us, no questions asked until after."

He heard a car door outside.

Marcus went over to the window and glanced out. "Karen and Jack are here," he said before striding back over to the sofa and resting his hands on his hips, dragging his gaze over to Brady. "So I'll leave you with this, young man: I stand up for what I believe in because it matters to me. I screwed up a lot. I had a head full of steam, and, as Owen has pointed out too many times, I was hell on wheels. But I was proud of that when I was your age. I still cringe, thinking back on what I did and what I said, but I cleaned up my act and got my shit together after a lot of years. Even though I'm proud of being, as people say, just an average guy, I'm always there for my family first. I'm a damn good brother, husband, father. If you get in trouble, I'm your first call, because I'm there, standing beside you no matter what. All of us are." He walked around the sofa and rested his hand on his shoulder. "You may not have the same last name as us, Brady, but you are an O'Connell, so don't forget that."

He heard the door open, then his sister's voice.

Marcus was still staring down at him. "So why don't you tell us about this girl you've been seeing?" he said.

Brady wondered for a second whether he was being followed. "What?"

"That's another thing about us," Marcus said. "We know everything that's going on, and we're in everyone's business. You think we don't know about that cute waitress you make eyes at every day at the diner? You stop in almost every day for lunch and take her out, and you think word wouldn't come back to us? Yet we haven't met her, so I figured it was time to sit you down so you understand how things work here."

What the hell was he supposed to say? This was his family, and they obviously knew about Cassie, but there was something appealing about keeping his love life separate from the O'Connells. He realized they were all staring at him, waiting for him to say something as he fought the urge to squirm under their scrutiny.

"I see you're having some trouble, Brady, so let me help you out," Marcus said. "Are you messing around with her, or is it serious?"

There were times brother Marcus became sheriff Marcus, and he felt the cop staring down on him now.

"Can I plead the fifth?" he said, squeezing his beer.

Marcus took a step back and shook his head. "Nope. So let's say you bring her around tomorrow night so we can meet her."

He wondered what would happen if he said no. No one said a word, and Marcus didn't move.

"Fine," was all he said.

Marcus stepped back and gestured to Luke, who reached behind his chair and slid a wrapped box over to him, saying, "Your other gift, young man. Happy birthday."

As he reached for the box, all he could think was that he'd been pulled into the most unusual family. He glanced up to Alison, who was following Charlotte and Eva down the stairs. There she was, the reason he hadn't brought Cassie around and was still dancing in the shadows with her.

Awkwardness still lingered with Alison, but maybe Marcus was right. It was time to move on.

"Lorhainne Eckhart is one of my go to authors when I want a guaranteed good book. So many twists and turns, but also so much love and such a strong sense of family."

(LORA W., REVIEWER)

New York Times & USA Today bestseller Lorhainne Eckhart is best known for writing Raw Relatable Real Romance where "Morals and family are running themes." As one fan calls her, she is the "Queen of the family saga." (aherman) writing "the ups and downs of what goes on within a family but also with some suspense, angst and of course a bit of romance thrown in for good measure." Follow Lorhainne on Bookbub to receive alerts on New Releases and Sales and join her mailing list at Lorhainne-Eckhart.com for her Monday Blog, all book news, give-aways and FREE reads. With over 120 books, audiobooks, and multiple series published and available at all, retailers now translated into six languages. She is a multiple recipient of the Readers' Favorite Award for Suspense and Romance, and lives in the Pacific Northwest on an island, is the mother of three, her oldest has autism and she is an advocate for never giving up on your dreams.

"Lorhainne Eckhart has this uncanny way of just hitting the spot every time with her books."

(CAROLINE L., REVIEWER)

The O'Connells: *The O'Connells of Livingston, Montana are not your typical family. A riveting collection of stories surrounding the ups and downs of what goes on within a family but also with some suspense, angst and of course a bit of romance thrown in for good measure. "I thought I loved the Friessens, but I absolutely adore the O'Connell's. Each and every book has different genres of stories, but the one thing in common is how she is able to wrap it around the family, which is the heart of each story." (C. Logue)*

The Friessens: *An emotional big family romance series, the Friessen family siblings find their relationships tested, lay their hearts on the line, and discover lasting love! "Lorhainne Eckhart is one of my go to authors when I want a guaranteed good book. So many twists and turns, but also so much love and such a strong sense of family." (Lora W., Reviewer)*

The Parker Sisters: *The Parker Sisters are a close-knit family, and like any other family they have their ups and downs. Eckhart has crafted another intense family drama… "The character development is outstanding, and the emotional investment is high…" (Aherman, Reviewer)*

The McCabe Brothers: *Join the five McCabe siblings on their journeys to the dark and dangerous side of love! An intense, exhilarating collection of romantic thrillers you won't want to miss. — "Eckhart has a new series that is definitely worth the read. The queen of the family saga started this series with a spin-off of her wildly successful Friessen series." From a Readers' Favorite award—winning author and "queen of the family saga" (Aherman)*

Billy Jo McCabe Mystery: *The social worker and the cop, an unlikely couple drawn together on a small, secluded Pacific Northwest island where nothing is as it seems. Protecting the innocent comes at a cost, and what seems to be a sleepy, quiet town is anything but.*

Lorhainne loves to hear from her readers! You can connect with me at:

www.LorhainneEckhart.com
lorhainneeckhart.le@gmail.com

facebook.com/AuthorLorhainneEckhart

twitter.com/LEckhart

instagram.com/lorhainneeckhart

bookbub.com/profile/lorhainne-eckhart

pinterest.com/lorhainneeckhart

The Outsider Series
The Forgotten Child (Brad and Emily)
A Baby and a Wedding *(An Outsider Series Short)*
Fallen Hero (Andy, Jed, and Diana)
The Search *(An Outsider Series Short)*
The Awakening (Andy and Laura)
Secrets (Jed and Diana)
Runaway (Andy and Laura)
Overdue *(An Outsider Series Short)*
The Unexpected Storm (Neil and Candy)
The Wedding (Neil and Candy)

The Friessens: A New Beginning
The Deadline (Andy and Laura)
The Price to Love (Neil and Candy)
A Different Kind of Love (Brad and Emily)
A Vow of Love, A Friessen Family Christmas

The Friessens
The Reunion
The Bloodline (Andy & Laura)
The Promise (Diana & Jed)
The Business Plan (Neil & Candy)
The Decision (Brad & Emily)
First Love (Katy)
Family First
Leave the Light On
In the Moment

In the Family
In the Silence
In the Charm
Unexpected Consequences
It Was Always You
The First Time I Saw You
Welcome to My Arms
Welcome to Boston
I'll Always Love You
Ground Rules
A Reason to Breathe
You Are My Everything
Anything For You
The Homecoming
Stay Away From My Daughter
The Bad Boy
A Place of Our Own
The Visitor
All About Devon
Long Past Dawn
How to Heal a Heart
Keep Me In Your Heart

The O'Connells
The Neighbor
The Third Call
The Secret Husband
The Quiet Day
The Commitment
The Missing Father
The Hometown Hero
Justice
The Family Secret

The Fallen O'Connell
The Return of the O'Connells
And The She Was Gone
The Stalker
The O'Connell Family Christmas
The Girl Next Door
Broken Promises
The Gatekeeper
The Hunted

The McCabe Brothers
Don't Stop Me (Vic)
Don't Catch Me (Chase)
Don't Run From Me (Aaron)
Don't Hide From Me (Luc)
Don't Leave Me (Claudia)
Out of Time

A Billy Jo McCabe Mystery
Nothing As it Seems
Hiding in Plain Sight
The Cold Case
The Trap
Above the Law
The Stranger at the Door
The Children
The Last Stand
The Charity
The Sacrifice

The Wilde Brothers
The One (Joe and Margaret)
The Honeymoon, A Wilde Brothers Short

Friendly Fire (Logan and Julia)
Not Quite Married, A Wilde Brothers Short
A Matter of Trust (Ben and Carrie)
The Reckoning, A Wilde Brothers Christmas
Traded (Jake)
Unforgiven (Samuel)
The Holiday Bride

Married in Montana

His Promise
Love's Promise
A Promise of Forever

The Parker Sisters

Thrill of the Chase
The Dating Game
Play Hard to Get
What We Can't Have
Go Your Own Way
A June Wedding

Kate & Walker

One Night
Edge of Night
Last Night

Walk the Right Road Series

The Choice
Lost and Found
Merkaba
Bounty
Blown Away: The Final Chapter
He Came Back

The Saved Series
Saved
Vanished
Captured

Single Titles
Loving Christine